THE SECRET OF
BRUJA
MOUNTAIN

Weekly Reader Books presents

THE SECRET OF BRUJA MOUNTAIN

by
Mary Louise Sherer

Illustrated by
Beverly Dobrin Wallace

HARVEY HOUSE, INC.
Publishers
Irvington, New York 10533

THE SECRET OF
BRUJA
MOUNTAIN

Chapter One

Rico Diego rested one hand on his shovel and pushed back his straight black hair with the other. His father came to stand beside him and together they watched the fires they had lighted around the base of their charcoal kiln. In the steaming jungle of Panama it was always good to rest.

"You have time to fill the sacks from the charcoal pile and load them into the cayuko. Then you'll be ready for tomorrow's trip to town." As if the matter were settled, Rico's father moved over to fan the flame in one of the holes at the base of the kiln.

"But I promised mother I'd help in the banana patch," Rico said. He stood on one foot and scuffed the other one back and forth in the damp earth. "And Father," he added, "the cayuko is leaking and needs . . ."

"The same old excuses," his father interrupted. "Every time I ask you to go where anyone will see you, there's an argument. Turn the good side of your face, if you can't stand people looking at the scars."

"Louis!" Rico's mother screamed at his father. "How can you speak to the boy like that? Is it his fault that his face was burned?"

"Yes. Yes, Maria," Rico heard his father say impatiently. "But the boy is twelve years old now and grown-up for his years. He must learn to live with his face. He can't always run away."

Rico dropped his sacks near the charcoal pile and stood still. Gently he stroked the smooth, brown skin on the right side of his face, thinking what fun it would be to go to town if he looked like other boys. Then he felt the puckered skin on the other side and jerked his hand down. My father would run away too, he thought, if his face looked like mine. Only this morning Rico had looked at himself again in the small mirror his mother owned. The ugly skin on the left side of his face was so shrivelled that it pulled one side of his mouth crooked and drew down the corner of his eye. It reminded him of the fierce masks worn at a fiesta. Wherever he went people stared and turned away. It had been seven years since he had fallen into the fire and he still shivered whenever he thought about it.

Rico plopped down on a log and kicked a rock out of the way. When he was little, his mother had said that the scars wouldn't show as much when he was older, but now he knew that he'd have them for the rest of his life. Anger lit up his black eyes. Why couldn't people leave him alone? Why couldn't father send José or Uncle Thomáso to town? José hated the jungle anyway and Uncle Thomáso was always glad of an excuse to stop work on the kilns.

Rico worked fast, his anger driving him, and soon he had six sacks filled with the crisp, shiny charcoal. When the job was finished, he felt better. Deep down he knew that his brother, José, wasn't old enough to take the charcoal to town alone. But Uncle Thomáso could do it. People didn't stare at him.

Rico walked over to check his cayuko. It wasn't leaking yet, but he wanted to go over the bottom of the boat with pitch just to be sure. He was proud of the cayuko. The long, slow job of hollowing out the big mahogany log had been his work; his father helped only on the pointed ends. Now his boat lay at the edge of the river, half in mud, half in water, waiting to carry him wherever he wanted to go.

Rico stacked the sacks along the fourteen-foot length of the boat and went back to the house. The family was already eating the beans his mother had been cooking all day over the steady charcoal fire. There was nothing better than his mother's beans with red pepper sauce.

After supper, José pointed to the insects that swarmed in the night air. "We better hurry or we'll be eaten by all those bugs." He climbed up the notched log that led to the upper, closed-in section of the house. The lower part was open except for a two-foot wall that kept out small jungle animals. The others were quick to follow. When they were all at the top, Señor Diego turned the log over so that no unwanted creature could walk up using the notches for steps.

Rico didn't remember falling asleep, but all too soon the booming, drawn-out wail of the howler monkeys announced to the entire jungle that the first rays of the morning sun had reached the tree tops. He got up sleepily, ate the rice gruel his mother put before him, and went out to his cayuko.

"Remember," his father said, "four sacks of charcoal are for Ah Wing at the cantina and the other two are for the Alcalde."

His mother came out to stand beside his father. "Where are your shoes?" she asked.

Rico hurried back to bring his shoes and set them carefully in the cayuko. He would put them on before reaching town, for only a *primitivo* would walk in the street without shoes and he certainly didn't want people to think him so stupid. Rico was proud that his father had taught him to speak the beautiful Spanish, not the careless language used by ignorant boatmen. He knew when to wear shoes, too.

His father taught him many things in the hour they spent together each day after the siesta. Rico could write his name and do sums better than Ah Wing. His father had taught him about the jungle animals and about the hardwood trees and how boards were made from logs. When they ate salt pork, his father told how the pigs were raised and the salt pork made. He learned of things his father had seen in the city, about rubber trees and what rubber was used for. When they sat down together at the table, Rico knew there would be something new and interesting to learn about. One time he had heard his father say to his mother, "I worry that the boys are not getting a formal education. I teach them as best I can, but it is not enough. Some things they know well and of others they are ignorant."

"You won't forget my flour?" his mother questioned. "And I need thread to mend your clothes," she added.

"Here is the string with the knot tied for each thing you are to bring back." Rico tied the string around his neck.

"Bring me a coconut molasses candy," José said, coming up to help get the cayuko into the open water.

Rico nodded, thinking that on this trip he'd sneak around back of Old Indian Pete to listen when the old man told his stories. There was one special story he wanted to hear over again. It was about a place far up in Bruja Mountain where few people went—a place where medicine men lived who could make people well. Indian Pete told about children who had been burned and made well by the medicine men.

Rico knelt in the boat to pick up the paddle and guide the cayuko forward. When he rounded the bend, he stopped paddling and let the cayuko glide on the slow

current. Silently he slid into a green tunnel where the jungle growth crowded close on both sides of the water. It was like entering a green room, dim and peaceful. The only sound was a constant hum of the music of a million insects.

Everything here was so perfect that Rico forgot about his problems. He sat back and wished he could slide along like this forever, looking out into a mass of living green where the trees were so crowded together that he couldn't tell which branch belonged to which tree.

Soon the green tunnel opened into a wider stream with less undergrowth along its banks. Hot sun beat down on Rico's back and the jungle steamed so that every leaf and stem dripped moisture. The sound was like soft raindrops and Rico sniffed the musty, wet earth smell. He paddled smoothly and the cayuko skimmed over the water. A sleepy owl muttered and monkeys chattered in the treetops.

Suddenly Rico back-paddled to hold his cayuko steady. He peered up into a nearby tree. Had something moved? He smiled to himself and noiselessly paddled ahead to beach his cayuko on the muddy bank in a small clearing. His bare feet made no sound as he searched around for good throwing stones. Then he sneaked up to the tree without snapping a twig.

Lying along the branches were three lazy iguana. About five feet long, the lizards were as green as the leaves. Rico would never have noticed if one of them hadn't moved. Their long tails pointed toward the tree trunk and the rubbery spines on their backs made them look like dangerous monsters. But Rico knew they would sneak away at the slightest sound and that the spines were floppy and soft. Their meat was better than chicken and Rico decided to take one along as a present for the Alcalde's wife. She always gave him something special to take home.

When he reached the right spot he took careful aim. Wham! Three iguana splashed into the water. Two disappeared immediately, but the third floated slowly on the sluggish river.

Rico ran to shore and was ready to wade out to pick up his prize when he heard a splash on the opposite side of the stream. Watching, he saw the familiar, triangular ripple made by the snout of an alligator. The alligator had seen the iguana, too, and was moving out to snap him up for breakfast.

Rico raced into the water and waded into the path of the floating iguana. He stopped, waiting for the current to bring the lizard within his reach, while he watched the advance of the alligator.

The ugly snout that made the ripple moved at him with direct purpose. The staring eyes never blinked. Rico's skin prickled. He knew it was a big alligator because of the distance between its eyes, and he had heard his father tell how a hungry 'gator would kill a man. Maybe this one was hungry!

Rico wished he had let the alligator take his breakfast. Fear gripped him as the creature came closer. "Go! Go!" Rico yelled as loud as he could. He kicked and splashed the water.

The snout kept coming nearer. Rico couldn't move. He stood paralyzed while the steady, bulging eyes came closer and closer.

Chapter Two

Rico didn't know how long he stood with the water lapping around his knees. It seemed forever. Run! Run! he told himself, but his feet wouldn't move.

As he watched, the alligator hit shallow water. Its huge, triangular head reared up. Rico saw the sickly white streak down its belly. The 'gator opened his mouth. It was like a cavern with long, sharp teeth parted to clamp down.

Something brushed Rico's legs and jerked him into action. He reached down, grabbed wildly, and raced for shore. Down the bank he ran, to tumble into his cayuko. He lay there trembling, still holding on to the clammy object he had snatched from the water. He looked at it with surprise. It was the iguana he had waded out to retrieve.

When he felt calmer, Rico turned to look back. The triangular ripple was still moving steadily, but now the alligator was swimming toward the opposite bank.

Rico blew out his breath and let the iguana fall at his feet. The Alcalde's wife would be pleased, but next time he'd see to it that it was the old 'gator who had iguana to eat.

Rico laid the iguana in the shadow of the sacks of charcoal and pushed the cayuko into the moving water.

The backward push of the current was strong as he neared Maria Blanca. The tide was coming in and it would be easy to cross the bar where the Río Indio emptied her waters into the blue Caribbean. Rico's knees dug into the pad beneath them and his arms strained to keep the cayuko moving forward against the tide. He was glad when he came to the shelter of the cove and could coast. Trips to town would be fun, he thought, if people didn't stare at him and if the kids didn't torment him because of his face.

Maria Blanca was a sleepy village set in a coconut grove with one wide street stretching to the water's edge. Only when a flat-bottomed lugger or a banana boat tied up at the dock to unload and pick up cargo did the village burst into activity.

As he crossed the cove he could see a ship moving in toward shore. Rico paddled faster. He wanted to be away from the dock before the lugger came in to pick up her cargo of coconuts. Everybody in town came to meet a boat and he couldn't bear to have so many faces staring and turning away in embarrassment.

Rico eased his cayuko over to the dock and pulled it up on the white sand. He carried one sack of charcoal and then another to stack them high up on the beach above the water level. When he picked up the third sack, he saw children racing down the street to watch the lugger come in. Rico hurried and dropped the sack by the others. When he got back for another load, the children had surrounded his cayuko. The small ones were naked. Bigger boys wore only long shirts, and one boy, older than Rico, wore tan trousers and shirt just as he did.

"Hello, Monkey Face," the big boy greeted. "You here again?"

Rico bit his lip and went on with his job.

"Monkey Face, Monkey Face, Monkey Face," the smaller boys took up the taunt.

Rico pretended not to hear and walked back and forth from his cayuko to the high sand until he had but one sack more to move. He shouldered it and started as before. The leader stuck out his foot and Rico went sprawling on his face in the sand. All the children laughed and called out louder than before. "Monkey, monkey. You look like a monkey!"

14

Rico jumped to his feet and grabbed the big boy. His arms were strong from handling the heavy wood for the kilns and he gripped the fellow's shoulders with such force that the boy cried out. "Let me go! Let me go!" he yelled.

Rico looked at the bully's frightened face. "You're nothing but a fat coward," he sneered. When the bully tried to run, Rico gave him a push that sent him sprawling in the sand.

The boy got to his feet and ran. The other children laughed and took up the words. "Fat coward. Fat coward," they cried and ran after the bully.

Rico grabbed the last sack of charcoal and threw it down with the others. He heard the pieces crush, but he was too angry to care. He hurried to the cayuko to put on his shoes. He hated that, too.

The aloneness he always felt when he came to town was strong as he went back to his charcoal pile to start carrying the sacks to the cantina. Before he started, he looked out at the lugger. She was close to the dock now,

15

coming in so fast that he held his breath waiting for her to stop. He could see the deck hand holding his coiled rope, ready to jump for the dock to tie up the boat. Over-anxious to slow the lugger's speed, the fellow jumped too soon and went splashing into the water. There was a shout, and the boat's propellers went into reverse. Water churned and men ran up and down shouting at each other.

Rico was frightened. He forgot about his anger and his wish to get away in his concern for the deck hand.

Still the lugger drove forward. More men crowded to the front, but before the reversed propellers could stop her, the lugger ran the length of the dock, scraping the piling and thudding to a stop against Rico's cayuko. There was a splitting sound as the cayuko shot further up on the sand, breaking the rope it had been tied to on the dock.

Rico was stunned. He ran to his cayuko. It took all his strength to pull it around so he could see the damage. His fingers carefully followed the crack along the side. It must be four feet long! He stood with both hands against the crack as though he would pull it together again. His precious cayuko was ruined!

Now how would he get home? And how would they bring charcoal to sell in Maria Blanca? It had taken almost a month to make the cayuko even after Uncle Thomáso had the log ready. It wasn't fair. That lugger had no right to come in so fast that she couldn't stop in time.

Rico looked to the deck of the lugger and saw men running about, talking and waving their arms. Angry voices shouted at each other. Men crowded forward and spilled out over the beach. The dripping deck hand came yelling at a fat, sweating fellow who waddled over to Rico. Because he wasn't wearing shoes, he must be a *primitivo*. Rico had little respect for him.

16

"What business have you beaching your cayuko so close to the dock? Don't you know the dock is reserved?" the fellow demanded.

Rico knew that the dock had been built by the banana company and that he had as much right to use it as the lugger. He knew, too, that everybody was allowed to use the beach. The Alcalde had told him so. As head man of the village, he would know better than anyone. When Rico came to town, he always stayed at the Alcalde's home and they had talked about this.

Before he could answer the fat man, the town's people swarmed around examining his cayuko and exclaiming about the carelessness of a skipper who had come in too fast to control his boat. Rico was so angry that he just stood there kicking up a cloud of sand with his left foot. He couldn't get out a single word.

"I see you have had trouble, Rico."

Rico looked up into the kindly face of the Alcalde. Relief rushed over him like a tide, but still he couldn't speak.

Turning to the lugger man, the Alcalde said sharply, "The boy's cayuko can be mended and, if done well, it will not leak. But it will never be as before."

The fat man smiled at the Alcalde and his voice was whiny. "I'll get caulking material to fill the crack. We'll take care of it. We'll take care of it," he repeated.

Rico looked at the Alcalde gratefully. He was so glad to have such a friend that he didn't know what to say. His left foot rubbed back and forth through the sand. "He wouldn't have fixed my cayuko if you hadn't come," he managed finally.

The Alcalde nodded. "You deliver your charcoal, Rico. I'll stand by until your cayuko is ready."

Now Rico understood why his father said the Alcalde was the fairest man in all of Panama. "Thank you, señor. Thank you," he said earnestly.

18

Rico had never moved so fast. More than anything else, he wanted to get away from the staring faces. He shouldered a sack of charcoal and walked quickly down the main street to the cantina.

Maria Blanca's one cantina was owned by a Chinese, Ah Wing, who stocked and sold all the items needed by the villagers from food to fish hooks. He and Indian Pete were probably the only men in the whole village who were not down at the dock.

"Ah, you have come just in time," Ah Wing greeted. "Another day and there would be no charcoal."

Rico placed the sack near the charcoal box. "You know my father would not let the box get empty," he said. His voice was not quite steady.

The Chinaman sputtered. "I must be sure. I must be sure," he said, but his eyes laughed. Rico relaxed. The old man said the same thing each time.

"I have more sacks to bring in, and my mother wants her usual order," he finished.

Ah Wing nodded and disappeared in his living quarters behind the store. Rico waited. He wished he could

hurry and get the charcoal delivered while people were occupied with the cayuko so they wouldn't notice him. But he always waited like this. Before long, Ah Wing came back carrying a teapot and two handleless cups. He selected four cookies from a showcase and they sat down for their usual cup of green tea. Rico liked Ah Wing and enjoyed these visits, but today he was glad when his friend stood up to finish cutting salt pork into square pieces. "I'll be back," Rico called.

Outside, Indian Pete sat on the ground with his back against the store building. Rico hesitated. The Indian was half asleep and didn't hear Rico stop beside him.

"That story you told about the medicine men in Bruja Mountain, didn't you say they cured children with burned faces?" Rico asked.

Indian Pete didn't open his eyes. He grunted and mumbled impatiently, "My story true."

Rico's heart jumped. Maybe the medicine men could mend his burned face! He ran to bring up another sack of charcoal, new hope making his feet light. When he came near the dock, he stopped. Two men were having an argument about the best way to repair his cayuko. Other men were giving advice, but nobody was working. When he saw the Álcalde, Rico smiled. The Alcalde was examining the crack, getting ready to tell the workmen what to do and paying attention to no one. When I get big, Rico thought fervently, I want to be an Alcalde, too.

He slipped through the noisy crowd and picked up one sack and then another until he had delivered the four sacks to the cantina. He tucked Ah Wing's receipt for them in his pocket and went back to the beach. People were still standing about talking but he paid no attention.

The two sacks left were for the Alcalde. As he set the second one down by the charcoal bin, the Alcalde's wife came through the yard. She had been at the dock, too, and had seen the accident.

"Men like that captain shouldn't be allowed to pilot a boat," she said. Rico thought she sounded as if she were scolding him. She talked on and on about the captain's carelessness. He glanced up at the sun. It must be late afternoon and surely his cayuko would be mended by this time.

There were still many people at the beach when he arrived. Rico stood back from the crowd, but the Alcalde motioned to him. "It will be dry and ready tomorrow," he said. "When you start back, you'll never know there was anything wrong."

"Yes, because you made them fix it, señor," Rico said gratefully. It was then that he noticed the tall foreigner with the boy. The man's eyes were the color of the water in the cove. The boy looked about twelve years old, the

21

same as Rico. He could tell that they were father and son. Both wore khaki trousers and khaki shirts. They don't look like mine though, Rico thought. Theirs are new and mine are patched and faded. To avoid having them stare at him, Rico climbed into the cayuko to bring out the iguana. "I brought this for the señora," he said to the Alcalde.

The strangers examined the lizard from its head to the tip of its tail and felt the flabby spines along its back. "How did you capture him?" the boy asked in Spanish.

Rico was so surprised to hear his own language spoken by the foreign boy that he answered right off. "Oh, I just hit him with a rock," he said easily.

"Wow! You must be a good shot," the boy said.

Rico couldn't resist telling the rest of the story. Then, speaking to the Alcalde, he told about the tree where the three iguana were resting and about the alligator who had wanted some breakfast.

"Gee," the strange boy said. "You sure know a lot about the jungle, don't you?"

The boatmen began to collect their caulking materials and Rico was surprised to hear the Alcalde say, "You will pay the boy five dollars, because now he has but a second-hand cayuko."

The boatman hesitated and looked off at the coconut grove that had furnished him with many a dollar. He didn't want to part with the money, but Rico knew he wanted to keep his trade, so he didn't dare say no to the Alcalde.

Five dollars! Rico had never before held all that money in his hand. It was riches! His mother could have a new fiesta skirt made of yards and yards of cloth with red roses.

Rico tucked the money carefully into his purse. "My father will come himself to thank you," he said.

"Come," the Alcalde said. "Rico has brought us a feast worthy of our honored guests." He led the way toward his home, but Rico dropped back and the foreign boy waited.

"I'm Michael Davis," he said, "but my friends call me Mike."

"My name is Ricardo Thomáso Diego," Rico said politely and waited for the boy to go ahead with the others.

"Dad and I are going into Bruja Mountain," Mike said.

Rico forgot his self-consciousness. "You are? I'm going there sometime myself."

"Wouldn't it be great if we got to go together?" For Mike, enthusiasm made all things possible.

Rico didn't understand this. He wanted to get away

23

before Mike stared at him like all the others. He walked on, going in front of Mike so that the good side of his face was toward the stranger.

"Do you live here?" Mike asked.

"I live in the jungle."

"If you're visiting the Alcalde, my father could ask that you come with us."

"I stay here only when I bring charcoal for the village."

"Charcoal? Do people barbecue?"

"I do not know this word barbecue," Rico said, "but in Panama all cooking is done with charcoal."

They walked on down the street. Rico watched the boy, noticing that they were almost the same height but that his skin was pink and white like the inside of a custard apple. Rico realized in wonderment that this boy paid no attention to his scarred face.

Mike stopped to stare at a clump of tall coconut trees. "How do you get at the coconuts without any branches to grab hold of?" he asked. "Can you climb up?"

Rico hurried to a coconut tree. "You hold with your knees, like this," he said, demonstrating the way to climb.

Mike laughed and tried. "It'll take practice."

They walked on. One of the children who followed ran up in front to get a better look at Mike.

"He doesn't wear clothes," Mike laughed, taking off his funny hat. "I wish I could give him mine, this helmet anyway. It's a pest, but Dad says I have to wear it."

At the cantina Mike stopped again. "I'd like to go in and see what kind of things are inside."

"We better hurry up. The Alcalde might have something for us to do," Rico said.

They caught up with the others just in front of the Alcalde's house.

"Rico and your son may have their meal with the

other children, if you wish," the Alcalde said to Mr. Davis.

"That would be swell," Mike spoke up. His father smiled and nodded.

Rico was surprised. He would never answer if the Alcalde spoke to his father.

"This is the evening of the turtle hunt," their host went on, speaking to Rico now. "We'll want to start as soon as the darkness falls."

"We'll be ready," Rico answered quietly, but inside he was jumpy with excitement. There was nothing more fun than a turtle hunt. Besides, it would be dark and nobody would see his ugly face. Now he was glad his father had made him come to Maria Blanca today.

ico saw the quick, tropical dusk settle while they were eating dinner. He hurried through his meal, anxious to be the first one on the beach. Mike, used to eating slowly, had scarcely touched his fried iguana and rice.

"I'll help Old Daveed get the lanterns ready while you finish," Rico said. He wanted to get away from the Alcalde's children. They always made him feel uncomfortable.

Old Daveed had six lanterns lined up on the ground and was busy cleaning the chimneys. Rico found a piece of cloth and together they rubbed and polished until every chimney shone. Next they poured in kerosene, then checked the wicks. While Rico trimmed the last wick, Daveed got out the carbide lamp to use as a searchlight beam along the beach. The Alcalde came out to help with the lighting.

"The tide will be at its lowest ebb in half an hour," he said. "We will need that time to take our stations on the beach."

Rico, eager to be off, picked up his lantern and nodded.

The Alcalde hesitated and put his hand affectionately on Rico's shoulder. "I don't think you weigh enough yet, Rico," he said, "to turn a turtle over on its back without help. Besides, if you don't grab the shell just back of the neck, it could give you a painful bite."

"I've carried pieces of wood for the kiln bigger than the tortoise-shell turtles," Rico said, straightening his strong shoulders.

26

The Alcalde smiled and Rico ran off to wait for the others.

Mike bounced out as soon as Rico opened the door. They ran down the one street of the village toward the beach. Except for what fell within the arc of their lantern, everything was in total darkness. Rico forgot his scar since no one could see to remind him of it.

"I never heard of a turtle hunt before," Mike said, "but I've got a turtle at home. He's so small he can sit on my hand."

"You have? I never saw one that small."

They hurried on. The night was still and peaceful. Rico noticed lights in the houses set back from the street and thought how different it would be to live in town. Here the houses were low and close to the ground, quite different from his home with its ground floor room all open except for a low wall. In the jungle they would be eaten with insect bites if they stayed up late enough to use a lantern. Near the water, where the town was situated, there was always a breeze to blow away the biting pests.

"My dad's been here before, but he never told me about a turtle hunt. Do you sell the turtles?"

"No," Rico said. "My people use the turtle and its eggs for food."

They were almost at the dock now. "Let's stop and take off our shoes," Mike said. "It'll be much easier to walk in the sand in bare feet."

"Yes," Rico was quick to agree. It would be so good to take off his stiff, tight shoes. "Let's put them in the cayuko so they'll be easy to find." It was like a plot between them. For a few steps, they squished the soft, warm, sand through their toes in silence. The night was black, enclosing them in a separate mysterious world.

Mike moved closer to Rico. "It's so different from a dark beach at home," he said, his voice a little uneven.

27

Stars were out by the time Professor Davis and the Alcalde caught up with them. Professor Davis was looking at the sky. "Never have I had such a magnificent view of the Southern Cross," he said.

Rico looked up and stood spellbound. He could count on one hand the number of times he had seen the sky at night. Always at home he was snug under the thatched roof of the upstairs sleeping rooms as soon as daylight faded. It was either daylight or dark in the jungle.

Now the Cross stood straight up in the sky with a streak of light behind it. "I could climb a coconut tree and reach out to touch a star," Rico thought. He would have stood to watch, but Old Daveed came up and pushed past them to reach his station on the beach.

"We have but two hours before the moon rises, and that will end the turtle hunt," the Alcalde said.

"I want to hunt with Rico," Mike said. "He knows all about the jungle."

The Alcalde laughed. "Well, I guess it will be all right. You'd better call for help, Rico, to keep the turtle from getting back into the water. It would be better to do that than risk losing her. I don't believe you can flip one alone."

Mike and Rico promptly forgot about the stars. Rico felt excited and proud. This was his territory and the Alcalde trusted him to look after Mike and to find a turtle, too. There was no sound but their own quick breathing and the steady swishing lap of the water.

"It's sort of spooky," Mike whispered after a while. "Do you think there are any turtles?"

Rico didn't answer, but he held the lantern low to the ground to search the beach along the water's edge.

"What do I look for?" Mike asked.

"The turtle makes tracks with her flippers. Look! . . . We've got one now, I think!"

Mike dropped to his knees to see better. "It's something, all right! Let's hurry!"

A pair of foot-wide paths about two feet apart led away from the water. Mike was still on his knees, crawling ahead with the tracks. Rico walked beside him. "Do you think it's a big turtle?" Mike whispered, getting up.

"Maybe thirty-five pounds," Rico guessed. "A turtle that makes tracks like those would reach about up to here." Rico reached down and drew his finger across his knee. "We'll each pick up two sticks to mark the spot where she buries her eggs," Rico said.

"These tracks are plain enough. Couldn't we just follow them?" Mike asked.

"No, because the turtle tries to fool you," Rico said. "A man could dig half a day if he had only the tracks to go by." They were so intent on the tracks that they almost ran over the turtle.

"There she is!" Mike gasped and stopped. The turtle paid no attention to them. Her flippers churned sand like a boat propeller whipping up water. The boys watched while she worked her flippers to dig a trench. When it was about eighteen inches deep, she settled herself above it and dropped her eggs.

Mike raced around her to grab up one of the eggs. Before he was clear, she started to work her flippers again. A shower of sand poured over him. He shut his eyes and blindly ran out of reach. Still with closed eyes, he shook his head and brushed his free hand through his hair. When no more sand fell, he looked at the egg. "It looks like a big white golf ball, but soft and warm," he said, gently stroking the skin that covered the egg. "Gee, there must be a hundred of them!" There was awe in his voice.

"Maybe more," Rico said, moving the lantern to see better. "Turtles aren't like other animals. After they lay their eggs they never see the young."

"But how can the baby turtles live without the mother to feed them?" Mike wanted to know.

"Most of them don't. The señora says that's why the turtle cries big tears while she covers her eggs."

29

"Tears?" Mike tried to get a better look at the turtle's head.

"The Alcalde says it isn't true, that the tears come to wash the sand from the turtle's eyes because she sends it all over herself when she works her flippers."

Mike walked around the turtle again, stopping every few steps to try to see, but still keeping far enough away to miss the rain of sand. The turtle paid no attention to the boys, but continued filling up the trench and flipping sand all around to conceal the spot. When he was back beside Rico he said, "Let's collect the eggs and take care of the little turtles till they get big enough to look after themselves."

"My people use the eggs for food," Rico answered. He turned the light around to get a better view of the turtle. "She's gone!" he shouted, and dropped his two sticks over the spot where she had dug the trench.

Mike forgot all about the sticks he carried as they both rushed after the turtle. She paid no attention to them. She was on her way back to the sea.

"There she is!" Mike yelled, and Rico followed to the left. They circled the turtle, waved the lantern before her eyes, stamped, and shouted, "Go back! Go back!"

The turtle moved off her course, but still worked toward the water. They raced around her, pushed the lantern close, yelled, and kicked up clouds of sand. Still the turtle gained.

Mike grabbed up a big piece of driftwood and tried to hold it in front of the turtle. She shifted her course to the side and got around the wood. Mike thrust it in front of her again and again and again. Each time she edged sideways, but gained a little in her trek to the sea. Rico became panicky. "Daveed! Daveed! Help! Help!" he yelled over and over.

There was no answer. Still the turtle moved forward. If she reached the water, there was nothing they could

30

do. Rico rushed to the other side of Mike's stick to keep her from moving sideways. The turtle still kept going, pushing against Rico's legs so hard that he had to jump out of the way to keep from falling. He was sure she would reach the safety of the water before the men came to flip her over. If he could get her on her back, he knew the turtle would be stopped.

"I'll have to flip her myself!" Rico shouted. "Hold the lantern as close as you can."

Mike grabbed the lantern and thrust it squarely before the turtle's head.

"Look out! She'll bite your arm!" Rico yelled from in back of the turtle.

Quickly he stepped on the shell just above her tail. She still pulled to move ahead. At the same time, he reached down with both hands and grabbed the shell back of her head. With one mighty pull, he jerked back. The turtle flopped over and lay fanning the air with her flippers.

"Yi! Yi!" Rico breathed out. "I did it!"

"Wow! That was neat!" Mike shouted.

From farther down the beach came other shouts. Someone else was trying to head off a turtle. That's why Old Daveed hadn't come when they called.

"Let's look for another one," Mike urged.

"We'd better drag this one above the water line first," Rico said. "You take one side of her tail and I'll take the other."

Mike hesitated. He wasn't sure about those fanning flippers, but when Rico grabbed hold, Mike reached down to take his side, and together they pulled the turtle to a spot where the tide would not reach. Rico stood up and raked his shirt sleeve across his damp forehead. "I'm glad it's a tortoise-shell turtle," he said with satisfaction.

"Why?" Mike asked.

"The Alcalde can sell the tortoise shell," Rico an-

32

swered. "I must have caught her just right to flip her over. I never did it before."

"Turn the light and let's look at the shell. My mother had a mirror backed with tortoise shell. It was dark brown with yellow splashes. I never knew where it came from."

They tried to see, but the shell was made up of so many thin layers that it showed only a dark mass.

"Let's go back and start over," Mike said again.

They walked the full length of their territory and were on the way back when they found the next turtle sign. "She must be a whopper!" Mike exclaimed. "Her tracks look like the treads on a tractor!"

"If it's a black turtle, she might be six feet long," Rico said. "They are no good, but we can ride her to the sea if we can stay on."

Rico started off and Mike followed close. The turtle came into the arc of their light much before the water mark, but this time Rico didn't wait to call for help. "Come, come," he called. Mike joined in. "Come, come," they called together. "Her eggs are too strong to taste good but everybody tries to ride her back to the water."

The racket didn't disturb the turtle. They followed her slow drag up the beach. At the water line the turtle stopped.

Suddenly the turtle worked her flippers to dig the trench. Rico and Mike scrambled out of the way of the flying sand. When the job was done she sat there for a long time. Rico was careful to keep the light high while they waited. Outside the arc of their lantern the beach was dark. Mike moved to stand close beside Rico, their backs to the water side. The turtle stirred and Mike reached out to take hold of Rico's arm. Far down the beach a sea gull screeched. Then silence settled over them.

"She sure takes longer than the other turtle," Mike whispered.

"Yes," Rico said out loud. "She lays more eggs, I think."

Again they waited, but Rico's voice had shattered the gripping spell of the darkness. Soon there were voices coming down the beach and in no time the others came hurrying.

"You found her, so you're the driver, Rico. You get on first," Old Daveed shouted.

Rico jumped on the turtle's back as she started for the water. The uneven movement sent him sprawling in the sand. Everybody laughed and shouted advice.

"Better tie a thread around her neck to hang on to," Daveed chuckled.

Lanterns waved, making arcs of light in the blackness. Men shouted and ran in circles around the bewildered turtle. She didn't know which way to turn. She would start forward, turn a little and try a straight course again, only to be turned back.

"Get on! Get on!" the Alcalde called.

Everybody mounted the moving turtle grabbing the man ahead around the waist for better balance. They

held to each other, swaying this way and that and chanting, "Lean boys, lean to the right—" When the turtle finally reached the water's edge, everybody leaped and went down in a heap, still laughing and shouting. A full moon pushed up over the horizon, making the beach as bright as day.

Rico started off ahead, conscious again of his scarred face.

"The hunt is over," the Alcalde announced. "We flipped one turtle. Daveed and his brother got one, too, and you boys got a ride for all of us."

"We got a turtle, too," Mike said. "Rico flipped her all by himself."

"Good for you, Rico," the Alcalde called out.

Rico slowed and waited for the others. "It wasn't hard," he said.

"You must have caught her just right," the Alcalde said. "Now let's go back to the house. Daveed and his brother can finish up."

"Our turtle is straight up the beach from here," Rico told Daveed. "I marked the spot to look for the eggs with sticks placed like a cross."

"I'll find them," Daveed said, and Rico was sure he would.

Chapter Four

There were no howler monkeys in Maria Blanca to tell Rico that it was time to get up, so he slept late. He washed in the shed and laced up his shoes. No one was around. Rico knew the Alcalde would be at the dock. If he hurried, maybe the children wouldn't be out yet. Rico walked fast. He wanted to ask the Alcalde if Indian Pete's stories were true.

At the dock Mr. Davis was uncrating a motor and attaching it to the side of one of the Alcalde's big banana cayukos. Rico stood back where he wouldn't be noticed and watched with interest. Mike's father was tall with fine hair like Mike's, only his was brown while Mike's was the color of a ripe banana. There were crinkles around his eyes and his every move was quick and sure. He made it look like uncrating the motor was fun, Rico thought.

"Hi, Rico," Mike greeted, coming off the lugger with his arms full of bundles. "Gimme a hand, will you?"

"Yes," Rico said.

Mike stood holding his bundles. "Where do I put these?" he asked.

"Stack them on the beach, far enough up so the tide won't reach. We'll cover them with a tarp until we need them," Mr. Davis said.

The Alcalde came from the lugger and he, too, was carrying bundles.

"Good morning, Rico. Did you have a good rest?"

Rico nodded. "But I am very late." He was about to explain, but the Alcalde and Mike walked higher on the beach to set down their packages. As they came back

36

toward him, Rico felt the familiar urge to turn his back or to run away. He made himself stand still and straight.

"The professor and his boy came to our country to visit Bruja Mountain," the Alcalde said to him. "It had been arranged that Pedro Lopez would act as their guide, but Pedro is ill and can not make the trip."

Mike reached down to feel the smooth wood of the banana cayuko, but the Alcalde went on talking. "Your father and uncle know the Bruja Mountain as well as anyone else. Do you think they might be willing to act as guides?"

Rico's heart jumped. "I do not know what my father will say, because the charcoal must be brought to the village each week," Rico answered carefully.

The Alcalde nodded. "I think that can be arranged," he said. "The professor would like to return home with you to talk it over with your father."

Rico looked at Mike and answered gravely, "I should like very much to take Mike home with me." Then, remembering his manners, he added quickly, "And the professor, too."

The Alcalde laughed aloud. "Very good," he said. "Now, go back to the house to get something to eat. Then finish up your business at the cantina. By that time, the tide will be right to cross the bar."

Rico hesitated. "Do you think Indian Pete tells true stories about Bruja Mountain?" he asked.

The Alcalde considered. "Well, you must remember that Pete is a teller of stories, but he did spend many years in those hills, so no doubt his tales are based on fact."

Rico was satisfied. There were medicine men somewhere on Bruja Mountain who could make his face well. Somehow he'd have to find them.

Rico hurried, his hopes keeping pace with his feet. I'll have a face like other boys! I'll have a face like other

37

boys! The words went through his head over and over like a song.

The señora had fried plantains waiting for him and hard rolls from the bakery, which he had never before tasted. They were good, but he couldn't drink the coffee she poured. It was too strong and bitter. At home he drank the juice of the wild pineapple or plain water. The señora drank the coffee while she talked. "How is your mother's banana patch coming along?" she asked. "You should soon bring fruit for the banana boat when you come with your charcoal."

"Yes," Rico answered. "Then José will get his guitar and my mother will have a new fiesta skirt." When he had finished she gave him three of the big disks of coconut molasses candy he had been hoping to take back to José.

At the cantina he took the string with the knots from around his neck. The first knot was for the flour. Ah Wing had packed it already with the salt pork, salt, garlic, and baking powder. But there were six knots, and he couldn't remember what the last one was for. Rico looked around the cantina trying to recall the sixth item he was to bring home.

"A new file to sharpen your uncle's axe?" Ah Wing asked.

Rico shook his head and walked around again. In a corner, partly covered with a canvas, were stacks of tan trousers.

Of course, thread to patch his clothes. That was it.

Back at the dock he found his boat tied to the big banana cayuko. Boards had been fitted across it to make two seats. Mr. Davis sat beside the motor and Mike sat on the other seat. Rico stepped into the boat and stopped. If he sat in the space left for him, Mike would be looking at the bad side of his face the whole way home. Rico hesitated, then squeezed into the small space on the other side.

"Say—," Mike started to object, looked at Rico and moved over.

A lump came into Rico's throat. He couldn't say a word, but he knew Mike understood.

The professor pulled the starting cord. There was a sputter, then a loud pop like the shot of a gun. Rico grabbed the side of the cayuko with both hands. The boat began to move. Then the motor settled down to a steady chug and he relaxed his hold.

He was amazed at the speed. Never before had he ridden in a motor-driven cayuko. At this rate, they would be home in less than an hour. It took him more than half a day to paddle to Maria Blanca. Mr. Davis barely moved the steering handle and the boat went exactly as he wished.

If I had a motor on my cayuko, Rico thought, I could go to Maria Blanca and back in a single morning. But it must cost a lot of money. Even the Alcalde doesn't own a motor.

Rico watched the gleaming sand of the beach slip past. The propeller whipped the blue waters of the cove into white foam that bubbled around the side of the cayuko. With the tide coming in, the intertwining roots of the mangrove trees along the shore showed clearly. A gentle breeze cooled the air and Rico sat perfectly still watching the palm trees and the houses of the village grow smaller and smaller as they moved ahead. "It is truly wonderful," he said in awe.

"What's wonderful?" Mike asked.

"The way the boat moves over the water, with nobody using a paddle."

Mike laughed, and the sound was so happy that Rico laughed, too.

"Maybe dad will let me run it, and then I'll show you

how," Mike offered. They changed places and Mike held the steering handle. "The motor drives the propeller that pushes against the water and forces the boat forward," Mike shouted above the noise of the motor.

Rico wanted to ask what made the motor go and what made all the noise, but instead he said, "Yes, I have seen them before, but never did I feel a boat fly over the water like a sea bird."

"On our boat we can go faster because we put the motor on the back to get more drive, but your banana cayuko is shaped like our canoe, so there is no place in the end to put a motor."

Rico listened carefully. Mike moved the steering han-

dle. "See, you move the handle this way when you want to turn in this direction and that way to turn it back. When you want to go faster, you turn it here." Mike moved the throttle.

He moved it a little more and a little more and a little more. Soon they were moving so fast that Rico didn't see the shore at all. He forgot where he was, caught up in the thrill of racing over the water with the freedom of the wind. Never had anything been so breathtaking, so perfect.

"Mike, you'd better—,"

The warning came too late. There was a crunching sound. The motor stopped dead.

Chapter Five

Rico saw worry lines in Professor Davis' face, but the big man did not speak. Mike teetered the boat from side to side. His father did, too, so Rico followed suit. Nothing happened.

"We're stuck in the sand," Mike said. "Everybody out and push." His voice was cheerful as if they had safely landed at a boat dock.

Rico and Professor Davis followed Mike into the water.

"We'll try to lift the back to free the propeller," Professor Davis directed.

They lifted and tugged, teetered and pushed, but the boat did not move. Mike dived under. "The bottom is sand," he said when he surfaced. "Let's try again."

They were out of breath when finally they worked the boat free. The boys scrambled back into the cayuko while Mr. Davis looked at the propeller.

When he was again in the steering position, the professor stood with the cord in his hand and looked at his son. "Power without control is always dangerous. Try to remember that, son." Mr. Davis pulled the cord. There was a sputtering sound, but nothing happened. Again he pulled and a welcome roar sent a flock of gulls to flight. "Think about that now," he repeated.

As the boat moved steadily forward, it came to Rico that there were many kinds of power.

"The Alcalde has power, too," he said.

"That's right, Rico," Professor Davis agreed, "but the Alcalde has wisdom which guides his power."

Rico looked back at his cayuko. He knew he wouldn't

have his boat now if it hadn't been for the Alcalde's power.

When they had crossed the bar and were moving up the Río Indio, Professor Davis cut the speed. They were entering the jungle now where stout liana vines laced the trees together. Often the tall professor ducked his head to avoid a low-hanging branch. The air was hot and humid. Parakeets fluttered in the trees, the red on their wingtips a flash against the dense greens. A toucan bird scolded loudly, calling attention to his black coat splashed with color. They passed the iguana tree, empty now and shiny with moisture.

As soon as the jungle closed around them, Mike jerked up straight and peered into the growth that lined the river bank.

"What do you expect to see, Michael?" his father asked.

Mike gave a little start at the mention of his name. The professor repeated his question.

"Jungle animals," Mike said briefly.

Just then a lizard skittered over the water along the shore, so near that Mike could have reached out to touch him. Mr. Davis slowed the cayuko and they watched.

"It's an iguana," the professor explained, "a different species than Rico brought in for dinner last night."

This iguana was about a foot long. It had small front feet, but big webbed hind feet that worked like paddles. It scooted along the top of the water and disappeared into the jungle.

"That's the first time I ever saw anything that could walk on the water," Mike said. "He didn't swim at all. He walked right on the top."

"There are many like him," Rico said. They got under way again and Rico could hardly believe how quickly they reached his home. He saw his mother and José waiting on the bank. His father was walking toward them. As soon as his mother saw that there were strangers, she hurried back to the banana patch so that only his father and José were there when the big cayuko slid into the mud slot where Rico usually put his own boat.

"Father," Rico said, "the professor would speak with you. The Alcalde sent him."

Mr. Davis smiled. "I am Professor Davis and this is my son, Michael," he said. "We are looking for guides to take us into Bruja Mountain. The Alcalde told us about you and your brother."

"You will come to my poor home where we shall talk?" Rico's father invited. Mike followed the two men and Rico came last.

When the others were comfortable, Mike sitting on the low wall and the men at the table, Rico squatted down in the corner partly hidden by the table.

"There have been stories about a tribe of White Indians living on the Bruja Mountain," Professor Davis explained. "As a student of the races of the world, I would like to determine whether or not there is such a tribe."

Rico's father said nothing. Rico knew he would learn more before he would speak.

"At one time a party visited your country and brought back some of these people for study, but there was no conclusive proof that they were a separate people. I should like to make a scientific study, if we can find them," Professor Davis went on.

"All of the Indios are very shy," Rico's father said. "I do not know that you will find them."

"We will have to chance that," the professor said, "but the Alcalde tells me that you and your brother know the mountain well."

"That is true. We hunt there and gather the ivory nuts in season," Rico's father answered. "In the past, we have gone there to search for rubber to sell on the market in Colón."

Professor Davis nodded, and Rico felt proud listening to his father talk so easily to the learned stranger. But then, his father had lived in Colón when he was a boy and had gone to school there, too.

"Rico, will you get your uncle?" his father said.

Rico started off. Then, without turning, he called back, "Will you come too, Mike?"

Mike slid off the wall and followed Rico. "Gee," he said, looking at the small clearing with the jungle all around it, "it's no bigger than our front yard. If one of those big trees fell, it would reach right up to your door."

45

Rico looked at the trees. "You're right," he said, measuring with his eyes. "I never thought much about it, but every year we clear a little more land. It is hard because the jungle creeps back."

Rico led the way along a path to where his uncle was cutting wood. "Uncle Thomáso," he said, "this is Mike. Father would like you to come to the house right away."

"Well now," Uncle Thomáso said, winking at Mike, "he must need the advice of an expert if he calls me from my work."

The boys laughed. Uncle Thomáso was always teasing and it was a family joke that he was glad of any excuse to stop working.

After the problem had been explained to Uncle Thomáso, Professor Davis stroked his chin and asked, "Has either of you seen these White Indians?"

Rico's father shook his head. "I have seen signs of the Indios along the hunting trail and have felt that I was being watched, but never have I actually seen an Indio on Bruja Mountain."

"And you, señor?"

Uncle Thomáso was more encouraging. "When I was in the mountains looking for rubber trees, I stopped to make camp for the night. An Indio came over the hill above a small stream. It was late and the light was not good, but I could see that he was light in coloring with hair like moonlight. I called, but he disappeared into the jungle."

Hair as white as moonlight! Indian Pete had told about that. Rico jumped up, then slid back into his corner. He'd have to go on this trip. That was all that there was to it.

"Do you think you could find that spot?" Professor Davis asked.

"Yes," Uncle Thomáso said. "The hunting trail we follow each year could not be more than five miles distant."

47

"Would you consider acting as our guides?" the professor asked.

Uncle Thomáso was eager to go. He would much rather wander around in the mountains than stay home and make charcoal. Rico's father was slower to answer. "We have regular customers for our charcoal," he said. "How long would you expect to be away?"

"How long would it take to reach the spot you speak of?" Professor Davis asked.

"Two days should do it easily, if we get an early start," Uncle Thomáso said.

"Then I think we need ten days at the most," Professor Davis decided.

"It's been a long time now, but I once knew a bit of the Darién dialect," Uncle Thomáso said. "It might be useful."

Rico's father had more practical things to think about. "And the boy? He will stay here?"

"Oh no. He will go with us, of course," Professor Davis said.

Rico's hopes rose. Surely if Mike goes, they'll take me, too, he thought.

"It is not safe to take a boy into the mountains who knows nothing of the jungle or jungle animals. We could not watch him every minute and there are many dangers," Rico's father said firmly.

They talked and talked while Rico sat tense, his hopes rising one moment and falling the next.

"But I promised the boy," the professor said finally. "Could we not take Rico along, too? He knows the jungle and the two would be together constantly. Your boy's knowledge would be an added protection for Michael."

Rico's father considered this. "I believe it would be better that he come along with us than that your boy come without him. Rico knows the jungle well."

Rico jumped up and Mike slid from his perch. They would have raced out shouting but for the next remark.

"Wait," Rico's father said. "We must first be sure there is enough charcoal. I could take in next week's supply when we go to town. On that trip we shall consider further this matter of taking the boys."

Professor Davis nodded. "Yes, we must return to Maria Blanca before setting out."

"How much charcoal is ready?" Rico's father turned to Uncle Thomáso.

"Ten sacks, easily," Uncle Thomáso answered.

Rico's father looked at the two anxious boys. "Go then, and bring the sacks to the loading platform while I see to other things."

Rico raced from the house with Mike following. Professor Davis' search for the White Indians fit perfectly with his search for the medicine men who could fix his burned face.

Chapter Six

The sacks of charcoal were loaded in the big cayuko when Rico's father went with the boys to the kiln. "This one is ready to seal," he said to Rico. "If you work hard, it can be finished this afternoon. Later we'll set the fires to burn while we are in the mountains."

Rico was disappointed. He had figured to show Mike around in the jungle. But it didn't matter too much now that he was sure he would get to go up Bruja Mountain.

After they had watched the cayuko on its way, the boys turned to go back to the kiln. Mike grabbed Rico's arm. "What was that? Something moved over there."

Rico looked in the direction of Mike's pointing finger. "Come, Coca, come," he called in a coaxing voice. Lazily a cat padded toward them.

"He's as big as our poodle dog!" Mike gasped.

"Coca is an ocelot," Rico said. "I found him when he was a baby. Now he is a house pet." Rico reached down to stroke the cat's golden head while Coca brushed against him for attention.

"I thought ocelots were fierce, like wildcats and tigers," Mike said, keeping a safe distance from the cat.

"They are if they're wild in the jungle," Rico said, "but Coca is a good pet. Without him the thatch roof of our house would be full of rats and mice. That's why my father lets me keep him. You can pet him, too."

Mike reached out uncertainly and soon the ocelot was rubbing against his legs, making friends. "It sure would be something to have an ocelot for a pet. Wish I could take one home."

50

Rico walked on but Mike stopped near a newly-felled tree. "Do you make charcoal of this?" he asked.

"Yes," Rico said. "Uncle Thomáso and José strip off the branches and then Uncle Thomáso cuts it into two-foot pieces. Then he chops them into triangular pieces about eight inches on the bark side." Rico picked up a chunk and tossed it away from the kiln. "No wood should be close when we light the fires."

"Is this the kiln we're supposed to seal?" Mike asked.

"No." Rico pointed to a kiln farther over that was eight feet tall. "My father and I are still working here. First we made this circle of solid wood by standing the chunks on end, one round side in, one round side out. That way, air can move inside the kiln—not too much, or the wood will flame up, instead of smoldering slowly."

Mike looked at the circle, judging it to be about twelve feet across. "It sure takes a lot of wood," he said.

"We start the next circle at the middle leaving a draft hole. The second layer is placed with the bark side set on the point of the triangle in the bottom circle. It helps control the air in the kiln. The next two stands of wood are the same, only each circle is made smaller than the one below."

"It sure is a lot of work," Mike said. He followed Rico toward the kiln they were to cover.

Rico pointed. "See those two kilns? They are already burning. We'd better get busy with the rest of the sod for sealing this one or it won't be ready to light when my father gets back."

"They look like giant coconuts cut in half," Mike said, still looking at the kilns, "and nobody would ever guess they were made of stacked-up wood inside."

Rico led the way into the jungle slashing with his machete to clear the way. "We must put on a tight layer of big leaves first. Shall we get them ready?"

"What are the leaves for?" Mike asked, trying to use his machete as Rico did.

"To seal the kiln," Rico answered. "If we threw sod and dirt right onto the wood, the charcoal wouldn't be clean."

"This is fun!" Mike was still trying his skill with the machete. "Let's pretend we're Morgan's pirates cutting the trail to sack Panama City."

"I do not know this Morgan," Rico said.

Mike laughed and soon Rico was laughing, too.

"We'd better seal the kiln first and you can tell me about this game when we are already on the mountain trail. If the work is not finished, my father will say I must stay home."

It was easy to gather plantain leaves. The bigger the leaf, the more space it would cover and the piles grew as the boys raced to see who could get the most leaves.

They left their shovels and machetes while they went back to lay a tight leaf mat over that part of the kiln not already covered with sod. When the leaves were in place, they went back to cut squares of the dense grass that completely covered the ground. The sod was heavy to carry, for it was wet from the ever-steaming jungle.

Mike pulled his arm across his forehead to wipe the sweat on his sleeve. Rico looked at his friend's red face. "We shall rest when we get this load in place," he said. Then he saw the fire! It shot out the side from one of the burning kilns. Rico jerked up, his hands grabbed tight to the straw mat he and Mike were using to lug in the sod. Sweat broke out on his face and his heart pounded. "Fire! Fire! Fire!" he screamed and his voice came out weak and strangled.

"Fire! Fire! Fire!" Mike boomed out with him.

Rico's mother ran from the house. She brought bamboo buckets of water to pour on the green wood José and Uncle Thomáso were already throwing into the spot where the seal had given way.

"Get the shovels," Rico shrieked at Mike, while he began to unload part of the sod they were dragging. When he could pull the load alone, he brought it up in front of his uncle, who skillfully pitched the squares of sod over the opening. The flames poured out. Rico's mother jerked the mat free and ran back for the rest of the load. Mike thrust a shovel forward and they both shovelled and shovelled more dirt as high as they could throw it on the subdued kiln. The smoke grew as the flames died down. Finally Uncle Thomáso shouted, "Bravo! The kiln is saved!"

The others stood around talking, but Rico picked up the piece of matting to hurry back to where they had been cutting sod. Fire always upset him. He was ashamed of the tears and he didn't want his mother to see how he was trembling. The ocelot came over to rub against him.

Mike looked from one member of the family to another, then followed Rico. "Wow! That was exciting," Mike said. "Does it happen often?"

Rico nodded. "Too often," he said, and his voice was shaky. He reached down to rub Coca's ear to steady himself. "When a seal breaks, air gets to the fire. Then the wood burns up into ashes and we lose all the work we've done."

"What's the matter?" Mike asked, noticing how upset Rico was.

"A fire out of control terrifies me," Rico said, looking directly at Mike. "I run so nobody can see." Without thinking, Rico's hand covered the ugly burn on his face. He felt the muscles jump and jerked his hand down. "This scar came from a fire like that. I had pulled a piece of matting over to help, but I stumbled on the end of it and fell into the flames."

The humming noises of the jungle insects came through to them. A tree frog croaked nearby. Mike reached down to pick up a torn leaf.

"Why didn't you laugh at my face or look away when you first saw me?" Rico asked. "Nearly everyone else does," he added.

"I didn't think much about it," Mike said.

"Most people can't stand to look at such an ugly face," Rico said, "and I don't blame them."

"No, I would not laugh, Rico," Mike said gently. "My mother was in a car accident. She had a scarred face for a long time and wouldn't go anyplace with dad and me." Mike twisted the leaf round and round be-

55

tween his fingers. "But why didn't the doctor fix your face? The scars on mother's face hardly show at all anymore."

"There are no doctors in the jungle," Rico said flatly.

"I'll bet our doctors could still fix it," Mike said.

Rico didn't answer and again the hum, as of a thousand bees, took over their world.

"I'll ask my father," Mike said, a little less sure of himself, "and when we go home, I'll give you the swell new machete he bought me to take on this trip."

Rico only nodded and said in a loud, rough voice, "We better get the kiln sealed or there won't be any trip."

Chapter Seven

The big cayuko brought Rico's father home. Mike and the professor had returned to Maria Blanca.

Early the next morning the party would be on the trail, but Rico was not to be one of them. His father had decided that his mother and José might need his help at home.

Rico tried to explain about the medicine men who would heal his face, but his father said that was nonsense, that Old Indian Pete told stories for the fun of it, and that there was no truth in them.

Rico wasn't sure. Old Indian Pete's stories sounded true to him, and the Alcalde had said that they were based on fact. Now, lying on his mat, his thoughts were bitter. "If my father's face were ugly like mine, he'd look for the strange men to see if it could be healed." Tears stung his eyes and he turned over to get farther from José. He sniffed aloud in his misery and his mother whispered, "Go to sleep, Rico. There will be other chances to go to the Bruja Mountain."

Rico almost choked trying to hold back the sobs. Even mother didn't care about getting his faced fixed. His hand went up to feel the puckered skin. It was wet with tears, and he couldn't stop crying. "All they care about is how much work I do," he thought. Well, he'd make his own plans. Father would be angry, but he didn't care.

The next morning Rico heard his parents get up and go down the notched log, but he gave no sign. When José awakened, Rico asked him, "You heard me tell father about the medicine men?" When José nodded,

Rico said, "I'm going to follow into the mountains and stay behind all day. I'll come into the camp just before dark. You tell mother after I'm gone." Rico folded his blanket and took his machete while José watched.

"I don't blame you," his brother said. "I'd try too, if I had your face. But I'd be afraid."

They waited together, talking in whispers. They heard the banana boat come in and leave again. "The Alcalde must have brought Mike and his father," Rico said softly. Soon they heard their father and Uncle Thomáso come in the house and go out again. They waited until they were sure the party was under way. Then Rico followed José down the notched log. They ate the morning meal while their mother was still outside.

Rico stood up. "I'll go to the kiln as usual and wait there until the others have a head start. Don't tell Mother till you come from the banana patch."

At the kiln, Rico dropped chunks of wood on the first layer so his mother would know he was there. He watched the sky, trying to judge an hour's time. It was still not daylight when he started off, but it was easy enough for him to follow the trail. The first part of it was familiar to him, for each year when his father and uncle had gone hunting, they'd let him come as far as the game trail.

Rico had heard his father and Uncle Thomáso talk about sticking to creek beds so they wouldn't have to cut their way through the jungle with their machetes. Now the creeks were dry, but the stones in the bed rolled and bumped when his step set one in motion. He thought the noise would echo through the whole jungle, so he slowed down to pick his steps more carefully.

The path he followed was a narrow trail leading south through dense trees that met above. Here was the grey of early morning where the air held the coolness of night. Dawn would come soon, but now the jungle was strangely silent. Rico shivered. He would have to be careful, because animals who hunted by night might still be prowling for a kill. He kept his eyes on the ground looking for tracks. The marks of a small animal could be followed by a larger, hungry hunter. Rico knew that jungle animals didn't usually bother people unless people bothered them first, but it was safer to be alert.

Soon he stopped to examine a pile of steaming spoor on the trail. A coati, he decided. They make good pets, but they also make a good meal. Rico walked softly, his eyes and ears straining to catch any sound of a bigger, stalking animal. He knew that the coati usually hunted its food in the daytime and wondered what this fellow was doing out so early. He walked softly, his eyes and ears straining.

At a curve in the trail he stopped and jerked back. There was a thrashing in the brush. Rico stook still, every muscle taut. Only his eyes searched. If the wind were right, maybe his scent wouldn't be noticed. It was all he could do to keep from running back.

Suddenly he laughed. His eyes had found the coati struggling wildly to free himself from a tangle of liana vines. Rico pushed off the trail to grab the little fellow's

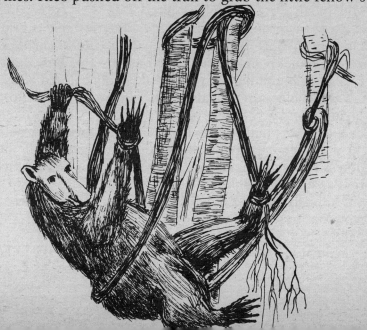

pointed snout to protect himself from its needle-sharp teeth as he cut and unwound the twisted vines. When the coati was free, it hurried off as fast as its awkward, bear-like gait would carry it.

Now the jungle seemed a happier place and Rico laughed again when the sudden booming yowl of the howler monkeys shattered the silence. A toucan screamed back, tree frogs chorused, and a flock of parrots flew up protesting noisily. Yelp, yelp, cha-cha-cha, they scolded as they took wing. Rico stopped to watch. They were so pretty and so much a part of his jungle.

More light filtered through the green roof, but the leaves were too thick to let in direct sunshine. Soon the jungle steamed like a hot bath. Leaves dripped as regularly as the drops of soft rain. Birds called overhead and above all, as though part of the air, was the steady hum of insects.

For the moment, Rico forgot why he was in the jungle and where he was going. It was so good just being there. For hours he walked, alive to every sound and movement, but thinking only that now he was on his way to Bruja Mountain where he would find the medicine men Old Indian Pete had told about.

Rico was brought up short when the trail opened up. He was so close to the others that he could hear their voices. Quickly he ducked back out of sight. Just ahead was a tree humming with scores of vividly colored birds.

"It's a blossoming balsa tree," Professor Davis was saying, "and a beautiful specimen."

A monkey, hanging by its tail and its hind feet, held up a flower cup to drink. Mike darted ahead of the others and stopped to look through a little box he carried around his neck.

The grownups stood watching while parakeets, woodpeckers, and hummingbirds greedily dug into the balsa blossoms.

Mike nodded. "I didn't know a balsa tree looked like

that," he said. "All my model airplanes are made with balsa."

Rico reached down to squish something crawling up his leg. The dead ferns beneath his feet crackled. He saw his uncle turn, then start across the clearing.

"I heard noises. I'll just check," he called back.

In a panic Rico dived into the dense ferns off the trail. He could count his uncle's steps—one, two, three, four—as he came onto the trail. Rico lay still. Would he see where the brush was parted? If they discovered him now, his father was sure to send him back. Desperately he listened while his uncle walked past the spot. Rico waited. Uncle Thomáso walked ahead a few yards, stopped and started back.

Near where Rico was hiding, on the other side of the trail, a band of monkeys was moving about in the tree tops. One of them dropped a handful of shells. Uncle Thomáso looked up and walked back beyond the spot where Rico lay.

Good old Uncle Thomáso! If he saw me, he won't say anything. He began to wonder about this. Uncle Thomáso was the best jungle guide in Panama and surely he would have noticed the parted ferns. Rico wasn't sure.

"Just a band of monkeys," he heard his uncle tell the others.

Rico knew he'd have to be more careful. For a time he sat there, weak with relief. He looked up at the monkeys. They were still jumping from limb to limb and chattering louder than ever. But their racket was music to him—they had saved him from being sent home.

As he waited, the sky darkened and the air became absolutely still. Every tree and blade of grass stood straight and quiet. Suddenly a clan of howler monkeys on his side of the trail roared out a protest, the heavens opened, and a solid wall of water burst over the group in the clearing. Rico sat sheltered on the jungle trail where he

61

could watch but not be seen. He heard Mike laugh as they all ran to huddle beneath a big-leafed tree. His father quickly opened a canvas bag to catch the rain, then ran back to the others.

As Rico sat near the trail, every leaf above him was a private umbrella on which the rain plopped and splashed, but left him snug and dry. As swiftly as it had come, the storm gave way to patches of blue sky, and the sun, like the searchlight the Alcalde had used in the turtle hunt, lighted the world.

Rico watched the others spread out lunch under the shade tree. His stomach was rumbling and his mouth began to water. He saw Mike put out hard rolls like the señora had served for breakfast. When he couldn't stand it any longer, he turned around and stretched out for the afternoon siesta. All of a sudden he remembered the disks of coconut molasses candy that were still in his back pocket. He gobbled two of them and felt better, but he wished he'd thought to catch some rain water for something to drink.

The sun's rays were slanted when they began walking again, steadily, steadily, until they were in higher country and the undergrowth was less dense. Rico was careful to stay far enough behind so that he could not hear the others. Then they wouldn't hear him either. Vines still climbed the trees and hung to the ground from the branches, some string-like, some as thick as the rope the luggers used to tie up to the dock, but now the trees were farther apart.

As it got closer to evening, Rico grew more and more uneasy. He knew he dare not sleep on the jungle trail without a fire, but he dreaded facing his father after he had been told to stay home.

Last night when he had made his plans, it had seemed an easy matter to follow and walk into camp when it got dark. He knew that he wouldn't be sent back alone because they were too far into the jungle. Rico had never deliberately disobeyed his father before, and the longer he waited, the harder it became to face him.

Chapter Eight

They had set their packs down in a clearing near two sheltering trees. Rico watched anxiously, trying to decide what to say. When he dared not wait any longer, he ran to his father.

"I had to come," he said simply.

They all stared. Rico couldn't tell whether his father was angry or hurt. After what had seemed an hour he said, "Your mother will be worried."

"I told José," Rico said.

The silence between them was a weight that Rico could not lift. He stood before his father, standing on one foot and scuffing the other through the dirt. When at last it was broken, his father said sadly, "I did not expect disobedience from my son."

It was Uncle Thomáso who brought them back to practical matters. "Well, he's here so we'd better put him to work."

Rico was sure now that Uncle Thomáso had seen him hiding off the trail. He knew, too, that no one would ever know about it.

His father turned and, without another word, chose the spot for their sleeping quarters. Rico joined in the task of cutting wood for the all-night fire. Uncle Thomáso was camp cook, so he unpacked the frying pan and coffee pot to start supper.

The two boys worked together and when they were a little distance from the others, Mike whispered, "I'm glad you're here. I felt like staying behind, too, when your father said you couldn't come."

Rico couldn't say anything. He nodded and went on

slashing brush, the feeling of aloneness welling up in him stronger than ever. He felt a stranger to his father and he had never felt that way before.

"Want to try my new machete?" Mike offered.

Still wordless, Rico accepted his friend's machete. They worked side by side, Mike's pleasure in Rico's presence a warm spot in an otherwise empty world.

Under the trees on one side of the fire, Rico, his father, and Uncle Thomáso built a lean-to of brush to protect them in case of another sudden rain storm. Professor Davis and Mike pitched their tarpaulin.

The smell of wood smoke and frying bacon filled the clearing. Suddenly Rico was starved and so thirsty he could hardly wait. When the call came for dinner, he was the first at the fire, Mike's machete still in his hand.

His father was standing talking to Uncle Thomáso. Professor Davis and Mike had not yet finished their shelter.

"Rico," his father said, "you have always been a fine son. It is hard for me to understand this."

He paused and Rico moved closer. "Father," he said earnestly, "I had to *try* to get my ugly face mended. I had to come." Automatically his hand went up to touch the scars.

His father turned his head and when he spoke his voice was gentle. "Yes, my son," he said. "And now shall we try to enjoy the mountains together?"

Before Rico could say anything, Uncle Thomáso pounded impatiently on a pan, the others came up, and dinner was spread out. There were quantities of bacon, beans, and fried plantains. They boys were looking for more when Mr. Davis stood up. "We better get the beds ready if we don't want to be stumbling around in the dark," he said.

Rico, his father, and Uncle Thomáso had only a blanket each which they spread out on piles of brush brought in from the wood gathering. The fire was in front of both shelters. Mr. Davis and Mike had camp cots and air mattresses. Rico had never seen an air mattress before.

"Why don't you try it?" Mike invited.

Rico lay down to test the mattress. "My own suits me better," he said. It was wonderful to lie in the open and see every tree branch outlined in the firelight. Rico thought of his mother and wondered how she was getting along with the banana patch and watching the kilns alone. He felt guilty leaving her with all the work, but he

66

knew she would understand. Now that he was on the way to Bruja Mountain, finding the medicine men that Old Indian Pete had talked about seemed more of an undertaking than he had realized. Unconsciously he rubbed his hand over the scars and started dreaming about the things he'd do when his face was normal again.

His thoughts were interrupted when Mike set his cot next to Rico's bed. They lay quiet for a time. Then Rico asked, "Why does your father want to find the White Indians?"

"My dad is a professor of anthropology in a university," Mike said. "He teaches about the different races of people. Some men are white, some are brown, some are black, some are copper-colored. They're all the same people, but some look different from others. My dad can't fit these White Indians in at all, so he wants to find out."

Rico thought this over. He couldn't see what difference it made, but he was glad the professor wanted to find out.

There were movements in the tree tops. "What's that up in the trees?" Mike whispered.

"Marmosets and Bruja cats, I guess," Rico answered. "They're about as big as ordinary cats and won't hurt anything," he added. "The fire attracts them, but most other jungle creatures stay away from a fire. That's why we keep one burning all night."

Uncle Thomáso grunted and Mike moved back under the tarpaulin. Rico couldn't remember another thing until he was wakened by loud yells.

"Help! Help! Help!" It was Mike's voice and he sounded scared. Rico jumped up. The fire was still burning, but now there were no leaping flames. He looked toward Mike's bed, but he couldn't see it. He hurried toward the sound of Mike's voice and saw what had

happened. The tarpaulin lay on the ground with Mike and Professor Davis struggling to get out from under it. Rico lifted it off. "Something landed on the tarpaulin," Mike said unevenly.

Professor Davis laughed. "It was probably a marmoset who got curious about the fire and dropped down to investigate. Michael jumped out of bed so fast he knocked out one of the poles, and the shelter came down on us."

"I don't think it's funny," Mike said, still shivering.

Rico moved closer to his friend. "Once Coca landed on our thatched roof and scared me like that, too."

Mike laughed uncertainly, "Your jungle is sure full of surprises," he said.

Rico's father got up and put more wood on the fire, but Uncle Thomáso only turned over and didn't pay any attention.

Mike's father put his son's mattress on the pile of brush and Rico spread his blanket on the cot. When all was quiet again, Mr. Davis reached over to touch Rico's arm. "You and I will make a jungle rat out of Michael yet," he said. The way he said it told Rico that Mr. Davis was glad, too, that he was with them.

Chapter Nine

On the trail the next morning, Rico swung along happily beside Mike. They were together in the mountains, and he was on his way to find the medicine men who he was sure could heal the scars on his face.

Daylight had not yet come to the jungle, so Rico's father bent low to look for animal tracks. He stopped and they all waited. "A puma has just passed here," he said.

"I don't think he'll worry us much," Professor Davis said. "He may follow and annoy us, but a cougar is a coward in a showdown."

"Rico's father said it was a puma, but you're talking about a cougar," Mike protested.

"We are both right," Professor Davis said. "The species is found throughout North and South America and has five different names. Because he has no spots, early settlers thought him a lioness and called him a mountain lion. He's also called a panther and a catamount."

Mike shrugged impatiently, "I wish we'd *see* some jungle animals instead of talking about their names."

Rico looked at Mike, surprised at his outburst. Mike was usually good-natured. As they walked along, Rico puzzled over this. "It's because his father always teaches," he decided, "and Mike wants to learn for himself. That's why he doesn't listen sometimes."

"Do you think we'll really *see* some wild animals?" Mike insisted.

"Of course," Rico said.

"You two should save your energy for something besides talking," Uncle Thomáso teased. For a short distance they walked in silence, each measuring his step to the man ahead. Suddenly there was a sharp crashing in the brush.

"Vaca! Vaca!" Rico's father shouted. "Off the trail!" and he leaped into the jungle growth.

Professor Davis, Uncle Thomáso, and Rico did the same. Mike was thinking about jungle animals and didn't hear. In a flash Rico saw this. He darted back onto the trail and gave Mike a hard push that sent him sprawling into the undergrowth.

Mike wiggled free. "What do you think you're doing?" he shouted and pushed Rico as hard as he could with his feet.

Before Rico could answer, a clumsy tapir came crashing down the trail, thundering past them without knowing they were there.

"What was that?" Mike gasped. "Looked like an elephant!"

Professor Davis reached out a hand to Mike and Rico and they pulled themselves back on the trail. Mike turned quickly to face Rico. "I'm sorry," he said. "I didn't even think. I just got mad. I should have known you wouldn't push me unless there was a reason," he added lamely.

The three men stood waiting until Rico said, "I know that, Mike."

Rico's father again took charge. "That tapir was crazed with fear. Must have had a cat after him. We must proceed with caution. Thomáso, will you guard from the rear?"

Again they walked in silence. Mike was next to Uncle Thomáso. "Do you think it was a jaguar?" he asked.

"Could be," Uncle Thomáso answered. "It's a good thing Rico pushed you out of the way. That tapir wouldn't have been so careful with you."

Now all ears strained for the slightest sound. Having witnessed the power of jungle law and felt the need to guard themselves from the hunger of a stronger animal, they travelled all morning with utmost caution.

Suddenly Uncle Thomáso stopped. "This is the spot where I camped the time I saw the White Indian." Pointing to a stream below a small clearing, Uncle Thomáso said, "He was just over that rise."

It had been a tiring morning. The creek bed they had been following when they had left the game trail was full of boulders and, since the flow of water was down the center, they had to climb over or go around every rock. When they branched off onto another game trail, it was one that was seldom used and they had to slash the jungle growth with machetes to get through. Rico had taken his turn with his father and his uncle and he was tired.

"We've earned a rest before starting off again," Uncle Thomáso said. He slipped off his pack and stretched full length on the ground. The others followed, and Rico lay down beside Mike.

"Do we eat before we look for the Indians?" Mike asked.

"Under that tree is a good spot," his father said, and they followed him to set their packs against a tree trunk in the clearing. While the men brought out lunch, the boys went back to the stream for water.

While Rico was filling the water jug and Uncle Thomáso's coffee pot, Mike darted into the jungle. Rico jumped up and raced after him. Mike was looking through his camera at weaver birds' nests swinging from several high branches.

"Mike, you shouldn't get off the trail," Rico shouted. "There could be snakes. You have to think before you act in the jungle, or you won't stay alive."

Mike snapped his picture. "I'll try, Rico," he said, "but what are the funny stockings hanging on that tree?"

"Those are birds' nests," Rico said. "We call them weaver birds, because the mother weaves the nest."

"I never saw a birds' nest that big," Mike said. "I wish I could take one home. I'd take it to school to show the class."

"Why not?" Rico said. "The nests are empty now. But don't get off the trail like that again."

Back with the others, Mike talked about taking home a weaver birds' nest.

"We'll eat lunch first and then look at it," Professor Davis decided. "You know, don't you, that it's just a bigger edition of the orioles' nest we have at home?"

Mike looked disappointed. "Well," he said lamely, "it's the biggest birds' nest I ever saw."

Uncle Thomáso was plainly irritated. He had come into Bruja Mountain to find the White Indians, and this was an unnecessary delay. "When you get up that tree," he said to Rico, "look around for a village or a trail."

Rico climbed the tree and sat in the crotch of a stout limb to look around. Below him the nests swayed as gently as cradles. Above his head the leaves closed in. "I don't see any sign of a village or a trail," he said, "but the leaves are so thick, I couldn't see if there were anything." Before coming down, he carefully removed the biggest nest he could find.

"Now what shall we do with it?" Professor Davis asked Rico while Mike was examining the nest. "It's too fragile to stand up on a jungle journey."

Mike was disappointed. "Anyway, I'm glad I saw it close up," he said, setting the nest down gently at the base of the tree.

After dousing their cook-fire, they followed along the edge of a stream. Now and then it opened up into a pool where trout and catfish swam. "Let's go fishing," Mike said, but nobody paid any attention.

Where the trail led over the stream, another path crossed theirs in an east-west direction. A branch trail also led off from the one they had been following. Rico's father stopped to consider the best course. "We should divide up and explore," he decided.

But there were four trails and only three men.

"Rico, do you think you and Mike could stay on the trail we have been following?" Professor Davis asked. "There should be no danger at this time of day." Then Professor Davis put his hand on his son's shoulder. "Stay on the trail," he said firmly. "And be back here within an hour."

Rico looked up at the sun and Mike looked at his watch. "OK, dad," Mike agreed easily.

"I'll take good care of him, sir," Rico promised. The two walked ahead, Rico in the lead. When they were out of earshot, Rico stopped. "You should walk ahead so I can watch," he said. "Maybe you won't remember to think first."

74

Mike laughed, "I'll remember."

The sun was hot and the jungle steamed. Side trails joined theirs, but they felt no urge to explore. A toucan bird scolded and they laughed back. It was wonderful to be together in the mountains.

Rico knew they had been walking a long time when he first heard the sound. It was a low moan as if of a creature in great misery. They stopped to listen.

"Do you recognize the sound?" Mike asked.

Rico shook his head and they stood quietly to listen again.

"Maybe father will know," Rico said, thinking they should not go closer without the protection of a hunter's skill.

They moved ahead slowly.

"We're getting closer," Mike whispered. "We should be able—"

In his excitement, Mike pushed ahead. The sound was so close now that Rico shivered. He knew that if it came from an animal, its mate could be near.

Rico grabbed Mike's arm. "We better go back for my father."

Mike took another step ahead. His foot went down. He yelled. Rico's grasp saved him from falling forward. The moan grew into a frenzied shriek. Rico hung on and pulled with all his strength. Mike fell back and scrambled to Rico's side.

"Run," Rico whispered.

They raced over the trail, not stopping to look back. Near the meeting place, Rico slowed down and they walked ahead to where the others were waiting.

Uncle Thomáso was talking. "The game trail I followed turned out to be a well-beaten path," he said. "We'd better see where it goes."

Then Mike told of the strange sound they had heard. "It could be a man who needs help," he finished.

"Probably a monkey," Uncle Thomáso muttered.

Mike was serious. "I'd worry about it for the rest of my life if we didn't find out."

Rico's father smiled in sympathy, but Rico knew that his uncle still didn't understand why they let so many things get in the way of their hunt for the White Indians. He wanted to get on with the job, too, but not until they found out who or what it was that needed help.

On the trail again, no one spoke until they heard the piteous moan. They stopped on the spongy trail to listen. The jungle steamed and dripped in the afternoon sun. To Rico each drip sounded like an explosion.

"We better stay close together, near the protection of the gun," Rico's father said.

Professor Davis checked his gun.

"Now careful. Keep your eyes and ears open." Rico's father led the way again.

Rico's heart hammered like the woodpeckers in the stump at home. He knew Mike was excited, too, from the way his hands kept hitching at his pack. A stone rolled. As one man, they stopped. There was no other sound and they moved on cautiously. The moaning was closer now. It was as if the creature had tired itself out and had little strength to call for help.

They were nearly on top of the spot when Rico's father put out his arm to keep them from going forward. The sound was just ahead, but they could see nothing and the trail went on as before. Perspiration broke out all over Rico. He stayed with the others, feeling as tight as a skin drum as he watched his father edge ahead a step at a time, stopping to listen after each move. Twenty steps. Rico could hear Mike counting, too.

His father drew his foot back sharply. "It's a game pit," he called and dropped down on his hands and knees to peer into it.

The others came up with a rush.

"There's a man in it!" Uncle Thomáso exclaimed in wonder.

The man was lying full length at the bottom of a deep pit. He was painted with wavy black and red lines that ran across his face and chest. His only clothing consisted of a loin cloth, and his skin was the color of bronze, like Old Indian Pete's.

As Rico looked at the Indian, he was afraid and sorry at the same time. Would there be more Indians, a whole tribe maybe, and would they be dangerous? There were still said to be some uncivilized tribes in the backwoods of Panama. But if they could tell him where to find the medicine men who could fix his face, Rico was willing to risk the danger. As he watched, Rico saw fear in the eyes of the man staring up at them. He tried to struggle to a sitting position, but fell back exhausted while they all stared down at him.

"We are friends," Uncle Thomáso said. "Friends, friends," he repeated over and over in the Darién dialect. Still the Indian was afraid.

"His leg must be broken, or he would have worked his way out of the pit," Professor Davis said. "We'll have to devise a stretcher to get him out."

"You boys find stout liana vines. I'll cut poles," Rico's father directed.

The professor and Uncle Thomáso cut notches in the earth leading down to the bottom of the pit. They anchored a vine to a nearby tree. Thomáso cut four small poles and split them with his machete to make splints. The professor got out his jungle first-aid kit.

As Rico's father cut poles and stripped them of their branches, Mike brought them to Rico, who wove vines in and out around them at the center to add strength and keep the stretcher from sagging. Then he tied the ends securely together. Six poles were bound in this manner with liana vines secured to each corner. Then they made a pad of big leaves and tied it on with smaller vines.

When all was ready, the professor climbed down into the pit. Holding the stretcher horizontally, those on top carefully lowered it to him. Gently he slid it beneath the injured man. Then he climbed out of the pit to take hold of a vine at one corner. Rico and Mike stood opposite and each of the others manned a corner. Slowly they pulled, trying hard to keep the stretcher level.

When the Indian rested on solid ground, he again tried to sit up, but he sank back, his round black eyes searching each face like a frightened animal seeking escape.

"We will have to camp for the night to give him proper care," Professor Davis decided. "His leg needs setting. And he needs water, food, and rest."

Uncle Thomáso brought the water jug. Professor Davis lifted the man's shoulders and he drank thirstily. After that, he seemed to understand they they were trying to help. He closed his eyes, and moaned only occasionally.

"Ask him how far it is to his village," Professor Davis suggested.

78

Uncle Thomáso's limited command of the Darién language required the use of sign language and many gestures, but finally he reported, "The village is about five miles farther on this trail, but there's water just ahead and a place to camp."

Just five miles to an Indian village! Excitement made Rico shaky.

It was well past siesta time so Rico's father and the two boys set out to get their camp ready for the night while Uncle Thomáso and Professor Davis took care of the injured Indian. The tree frog chorus was the loudest sound in the jungle as they started for the camp.

"It's funny how they can all stop and start at the same time," Mike said.

Rico's thoughts were still with Professor Davis. He wished he could stay and watch, but he knew there was too much to do.

The wood was stacked for the night's fire and they were building the lean-to when Uncle Thomáso came into camp carrying the Indian on his back. Professor Davis had their pack sacks and the stretcher.

Without a word, Mike dropped his load of brush and ran to open up his camp cot and help Uncle Thomáso lower the man to the bed. Then he got out his blanket and spread it over the cot. When Uncle Thomáso said, "We'll get him under the shelter of the lean-to," Mike manned one end of the stretcher to help carry him in.

Professor Davis was pleased. "I believe I've lost a small boy and gained a partner," he said.

Rico understood and smiled. He and his father had been partners for as long as he could remember.

Chapter Ten

The next morning the Indian was better, but still too weak to stand. Everyone except Mike carried one corner of the stretcher. Rico, being smaller, had to take extra steps to keep up. It was a relief when the trail narrowed and his father or Uncle Thomáso carried the Indian on his back.

By the time they reached the village, Rico was tired. Professor Davis made the injured man comfortable, then came to stand beside the boys. "You did a good job, Rico," he said. "That was a rough five miles."

Rico felt better after that and when he looked around, curiosity took the place of all other feelings. The village was only a clearing in the jungle. A dozen pole huts huddled together. Behind some of them were patches of corn growing as tall as boys, and poles with climbing beans. Cooking fires were burning, but not one person was in sight. Everywhere it looked as if people had left hurriedly. Corn meal and meat still bubbled in iron pots over the fires. Not even a dog protested their arrival, and Rico knew that dogs and an Indian village in Panama went together.

"They must have left in a hurry," Professor Davis said. "I wonder why?"

"To them a stranger is an enemy," Rico's father explained. "The early Spaniards taught them that and they are suspicious of all foreigners."

"Yes, of course," the professor nodded in understanding. "We must tell them that we are not Spaniards."

"Why?" Mike asked.

"The early Spaniards were cruel and brutal to the

natives," his father explained. "They wanted gold, and they killed and stole to satisfy their greed."

Before Mike could ask another question, the injured Indian began a frantic yell. The sound was terrifying and it made prickles race down Rico's back. Professor Davis hurried to where the man lay. The yelling went on, but with pauses between. Nobody spoke, and the silent intervals were as tense and startling as the man's wild cries. Rico didn't know how long they waited. The jungle and his whole body vibrated with the sound. He wondered if it might be a signal for the Indians to attack.

"This has gone far enough," Professor Davis said. "Ask him what he is doing," he said to Uncle Thomáso.

Uncle Thomáso nodded, but made no move to interrupt the yelling Indian. Mike reached out and took a tight hold on Rico's arm. Again they listened. The sound was a command, a pleading wail, an angry scold that began, ended, and went on again.

Professor Davis moved impatiently. Uncle Thomáso held up his hand for silence. "He is calling his people," he whispered to the professor.

It seemed an hour before they heard a timid answering voice. The Indian listened, then repeated the same cry over and over.

"He is telling his people that we are friends," Uncle Thomáso explained more easily now.

After much coaxing, a sturdy Indian came out of the jungle onto the trail. He moved toward them warily, darting frightened glances from one to the other. "He acts like a wild animal," Rico said, feeling sorry for the man. All the while, the injured man kept talking.

At close range Rico could see that this man's face was marked with similar black and red paint with a leaf design between the lines. The second Indian examined the bandaged leg. Convinced then that there was no danger, he, too, began the wild calling.

Soon all the people in the village—men, women, and children—milled around them. Rico wished he could run back into the jungle where they wouldn't have to see his face. They hurried from Professor Davis to Rico, to Mike, to Uncle Thomáso, and to Rico's father.

The children pointed to Mike's hair and to Rico's face. Rico bit his lip and turned away. But there was no way to avoid the eyes staring at them. Then he made himself stand straight with his hands at his sides.

These people were different from the Indians he had seen in Maria Blanca. It was plain that they had never before seen people outside their own tribe. It didn't seem strange to Rico, however, for he knew that Bruja

83

Mountain was a world apart and that each Indian tribe had its own hunting grounds. Indian Pete had told about that.

Rico looked from the painted faces to the long, coarse, black hair of the Indians. A few had the front cut in straight bangs. They were naked except for loin cloths. The young children wore no clothes at all. The women's hair was smooth in front and hung in braids. Sack-like shirts reached below their knees. In the nose of each was a silver ring.

Once they lost their shyness, the children felt of Mike's fine hair, pointed to the sun, then, laughing and chattering together, they compared it with their own. Next they pointed to his eyes and his fair skin.

"I feel like a monkey in the zoo. Somebody hand me a banana," Mike laughed.

It was different with Rico. He wanted to run away when the Indian children turned their attention to him and jabbered to each other. But he forced himself to bear their stares, and was grateful when they turned their attention elsewhere.

Excitement was still high when the man who had first appeared from the jungle raised his hand for attention. Everyone listened closely and when he had finished speaking, the women hurried away, taking the older children with them.

Uncle Thomáso explained. "The speaker is the village chief and the Indian with the broken leg is his son. The game pit must have been dug by hunters, and the son fell in it on his way back from another village. Since we have helped him," he went on, "they want to prepare a feast and make us members of their tribe. It is a great honor. To refuse would be to insult them."

Professor Davis welcomed the chance to study the Indians at close range. "Tell the chief we are pleased to accept his hospitality," he said. "Tell him also that we

have come to find the White Indians. Perhaps he will help us."

The chief was silent when he heard the request. After some thought, he agreed to show them how to get to the village of the *Moon Men*.

Rico's heart jumped and his hand went to his face. *Moon Men!* Indian Pete had called the tribe of the medicine men by that name!

The chief pointed to the far end of the clearing and everyone pitched in to help set up camp. When the work was finished, the Indians disappeared without a word, leaving the visitors to settle down for an afternoon siesta.

Rico and Mike lay near each other. "What do you think they'll do when they make us members of the tribe?" Mike asked.

"I don't know," Rico answered. "Maybe they'll test us to see how straight we can shoot an arrow from a blow gun."

"What's a blow gun?"

"It's a length of reed, sometimes bamboo. You blow darts through it."

"Like our bean shooters," Mike guessed, "but I don't see how they can hunt with a gun like that."

"Up close it's all right," Rico said, "because they use poison darts."

"You two had better rest or you won't be awake for the festivities," Professor Davis interrupted.

The next thing Rico knew, the chief was calling them to make ready for the ceremonies. If they were to be members of the tribe, they must wear its mark painted on their faces.

They trooped back to the village where three Indian women waited. Each had gourds containing black and red paint. The men took off their shirts and the women went to work, laughing and giggling. Rico and Mike watched as each new line changed the appearance of their elders.

"My dad will look the funniest," Mike laughed. "His skin is light so the paint shows more."

"Uncle Thomáso looks fierce," Rico said. "I'd be afraid if I met him alone on the trail."

Fancy circles were painted all over Professor Davis' face and chest. Uncle Thomáso had snakes and frogs, while Rico's father had a feather design to make him more attractive.

"Do you think the paint will wash off?" Mike giggled.

"I don't know. It's probably made of berries. They stain but come off if you scrub hard enough," Rico said. "I hope they don't paint us like that," he mumbled. The thought had been nagging at him and the worry of having them work paint onto his face was almost more than he could bear. Before he had time to hide, however, one of the women motioned him to sit on the wood block before her. Rico dared not refuse. He clenched his fists and closed his eyes tight. Then he held his breath as long as he could. Eventually he had to let it out and breathe normally. He peeked at the woman who worked the paint into his skin. Her fingers were gentle but firm and if she felt pity or scorn at his rough scars, she did not show it. Soon he bore the imprint of red lips painted here and there on his face and chest. Mike's artist decorated him with circles resembling eyes.

"You sure look funny," Mike said, "and I probably look worse."

Rico looked at Mike. Then he looked down at the lip-shaped designs on his chest. He smiled broadly and relaxed.

Wood blocks placed side by side formed a half circle around the chief. An Indian ushered each guest to his block. Then the younger women served large helpings of

corn cakes with meat centers, plantains, and wild yams. Plantain leaves served as dishes and fingers took the place of forks. Rico and Mike ate hungrily. They had had no food since breakfast.

"It sure is good," Mike said. "Do you think we could have some more?"

As though she understood, the Indian girl serving them brought more. When she had scooped a big serving onto each boy's leaf, she licked her fingers and laughed.

Around them the Indians sat cross-legged on the ground in the circle eating and drinking from gourds. They laughed and joked with each other, all the time watching their guests with open curiosity.

"They think we're funny looking," Mike said.

When the feast was over, the talking stopped and the children squatted down instead of running about. Slowly the chief began to speak, not only with his voice, but with his whole body. A violent shrieking was followed by a piteous whisper while the man rolled his eyes, jumped into the air, or dropped to his knees. It went on so long that the boys grew restless.

"Be still," Uncle Thomáso whispered sharply. "He's talking to the Spirits."

The speech ended with a mighty shout. Every member of the tribe jumped up and joined in a yell that Rico thought must frighten all the animals in the jungle. It went on until the visitors got up and joined in.

Wrestling matches came next and the enthusiasm of the watching Indians was greater than that of the two struggling men.

"They don't have any rules, I guess," Mike said, watching one Indian rub the other's face in the dirt.

"But they have fun," Rico said. "See? They are both laughing."

A race for boys was ready to start when the chief came over and motioned Rico and Mike to join in. Mike jumped up eagerly, but Rico hung back. He wasn't used to doing things with others. The chief insisted and the two lined up with the village boys, who were pushing and shoving each other to get the best positions.

A boom from the drum sent them flying. The Indians lined up on one side, cheering wildly. Mike shot out in front and Rico felt the tension of the watchers. Instinctively he knew that they didn't want an outsider to win. Rico raced by his father and heard his urgent shout. "Lose! Lose!" but Mike was too intent on staying ahead to have heard.

In a flash, Rico knew he'd have to keep Mike from coming in first. To be swift was matter of tribal pride, so their hosts wouldn't like having a stranger win over one of their own. It was important to keep the Indians friendly.

Using all his strength, Rico raced even with his friend. "Lose, Mike! Lose!"

At first Mike paid no attention, Rico bumped his arm and yelled again. "Lose! Please, Mike!"

Mike faltered as Rico fell back. It was just enough. An Indian boy shot over the line. The winner!

The crowd went wild. Mike stood where he had
finished the race, looking bewildered and disappointed.

Rico's father hurried up to him. "Good boy, Mike.
You won for all of us!"

Mike looked at Rico quizzically. "They didn't want
an outsider to come in first, Mike," Rico explained,
"and we want to keep them friendly."

Mike laughed, his disappointment forgotten. "And
Michael Davis threw the race," he teased.

Rico didn't understand, but answered seriously,
"Winning isn't always the most important."

Chapter Eleven

The next morning they made ready to continue the search for the White Indians. Their host had other ideas.

"You stay," he said. "You stay and we will have another feast and contests. Maybe this time your boy will win."

Thomáso was getting better at the language. It didn't take him as long as before to tell them what was said.

The chief looked toward Rico and Mike. They stood with the Indian boy who had won last night's race. He was showing them his blow gun and sheaf of poisoned darts.

No argument persuaded Professor Davis. He was anxious to continue on. After much discussion, during which Uncle Thomáso grew more and more impatient, a runner was sent ahead to advise the chief of the *Moon Men* that another leader would visit them and bring friends from a foreign land.

Again the Indian spoke and Thomáso explained. "*Moon Men* are weaklings," he interpreted. "The sun makes them blind and burns their bodies so that they must stay sheltered until dark. They are timid like the deer."

The professor wanted to ask more questions but the chief squatted in sullen silence. Rico sensed that he was offended because they wanted to leave his village for the *Moon Men*.

By mid-morning they were on the trail, the chief in the lead instead of Rico's father. Since the best travelling hours had been lost, the hot, moisture-filled air now pressed down like a stifling blanket. They had gone less than a mile, when Rico felt the straps of his pack burn into his shoulders. His head throbbed in rhythm to his steps and he struggled to keep from calling to his father to stop for a rest. The sulky Indian leader loped along easily and Rico knew it was a matter of pride with him to show no weakness.

Mike knows that, too, Rico thought. He learned it from the race last night, so he won't say he's tired either. They plodded on until Rico saw Mike hesitate and drag his arm across his forehead. "Isn't it time for a rest?" he asked.

Professor Davis looked back at the two boys and nodded. "Thomáso," he said, "tell the worthy chief that I must explain to him the care of his son in the next few weeks; that I would do this before we must think of other matters."

Immediately the chief settled down to listen and the rest of the party halted for rest. After that, it was the chief who would suddenly stop, settle his back against a shade tree, and relax.

Siesta time found them approaching the camp of the White Indians. Rico's spirits rose. He forgot about the weary miles behind them. The chief's steps were faster now and Rico was glad to hurry. At the edge of the clearing the chief stopped. He cupped his hands about his mouth and shouted. There was no answer.

"He expected their chief to send a welcoming party," Thomáso said. "His pride is hurt that they did not."

The village was deserted. Sagging straw huts set at random within a tiny clearing were weather-beaten and forlorn. No cooking fires burned; there was no sign that the people had moved in haste.

Their Indian guide was angry. He strode around the village making as much noise as he could and repeating the same call. The whole party followed him through one empty hut after another. The roofs were so low that

only Rico and Mike could stand upright. A thatch of split palm fronds formed the sides as well as the roofs of the floorless huts, making them little more than a shelter from the rain. Only one dwelling was different. It was built about three feet off the ground. The sides were made of small bamboo poles laced together with liana vines and plastered with mud on the outside. Rico and Mike climbed its notched ladder. Mike stopped. The inside was bare. "It's got a good floor," he said, and stooped to examine the halved palm trees, smooth and of one size.

"This must be the chief's house," Rico said.

The chief scratched his head and spoke again.

"He is puzzled," Thomáso said, "because we have not met his runner returning."

They walked around the clearing, the chief calling as they went. Only a noisy toucan bird screamed back. When he was satisfied that the place was entirely deserted, the chief led them back to the center of the village and squatted down to talk. The others sat on the ground around him.

"He says the *Moon Men* don't plant corn like good Indios. One day they hunt here, one day there, so they don't have one permanent place to live," Uncle Thomáso interpreted.

Professor Davis nodded and they all waited for the Indian to go on.

Rico watched his uncle and saw the crinkles come around his eyes. "Our host thinks there is no reason why we should not return to his village and enjoy ourselves," Uncle Thomáso said.

"It is too late to return to his village tonight," the professor objected.

Thomáso pointed this out, and the chief nodded. It was plain that today or tomorrow made little difference.

"Ask him whether the White Indians are a separate tribe," the professor prompted.

Before Thomáso finished his question, the Indian grunted, then spoke.

"He says many tribes have White Indians."

"Then how do they happen to live in a group by themselves?" the professor asked.

Before Thomáso could speak again, the chief got to his feet quickly, tapped his blow gun, and rubbed his stomach. Uncle Thomáso laughed. "He's going hunting for food, and we better get our camp set up, or it will be dark."

Rico and Mike were eager to go hunting with the chief. As though understanding this, he motioned to the boys. They scrambled up and followed his long strides. He led them back over the same trail until they came to a spot where it crossed a stream. Here they branched off and stumbled along the stream bed. Soon the chief stopped and squatted. They waited. Just ahead was a tree where a dozen or more birds, as big as good-sized hens, were roosting.

"Wild turkeys?" Mike whispered. The chief shook his head and motioned for silence. A hunt was no place for talk.

They edged their way to within twenty feet of the tree. The chief placed one of the darts in the bottom of his gun and raised it to his lips. Poof! The dart sailed through the air and landed squarely in the breast of one of the birds.

"Wow!" Mike burst out. "What a shot!"

Again the chief motioned impatiently. In a few minutes the bird dropped to the ground without disturbing any of the others. The chief took aim again. The second bird followed the first, then a third. With a satisfied grunt, the chief handed the gun to Mike. Mike took careful aim. Foo! The dart fell to the ground at least ten feet short of the tree. Rico's try was even farther from the target.

With a satisfied grunt the chief took back his gun and

went over to pick up the game. Frightened birds flying about made the air alive, but the three with the darts lay still. Without fuss, the chief pulled out the darts and put them back in the sheath. With the same ease, he wrung the neck of each bird as he picked it up. Holding the birds by the feet, he led the way back.

They were still travelling the creek bed when Mike stopped and pointed. "See those piles of stone and the fallen buildings? I'll bet they're old ruins!"

Rico looked and saw heaps of rock overgrown with vines and tumbling walls of stone half-hidden by jungle growth.

The chief stopped to look, too. "Bruja! Bruja!" he said forcefully.

"Bruja means *witch*," Rico said. "He's telling us to stay away, that spirits live in the ruins."

"Bruja! Bruja!" the chief said again. He shook his head up and down to emphasize his warning. "Bruja! Bruja!"

"I'd sure like to poke around," Mike said.

The chief started on, still repeating his warning.

"I've read in books about old ruins in Panama," Mike said. "You can find all sorts of things. Maybe tomorrow my dad will come back with us." He sounded hopeful.

Rico scarcely heard. He was thinking that maybe this would be a good place to look for the *Moon Men*.

Daylight was almost gone. Where the jungle was thick, there were black pockets. The chief walked faster and Rico and Mike almost ran to keep up. It was dark when they reached the camp. The whole clearing was in an uproar and ablaze with light.

White Indians! They swarmed everywhere, their painted bodies gleaming in the light of flaming torches. Rico and Mike stopped. The strangeness of these people held them fascinated. Voices, all loud with excitement, flowed over them. The chief hesitated, then strode to

where the camp had been set up and his runner stood
waiting.

Rico was so surprised and startled that he forgot
about himself until an Indian child pointed at him. Then
his hand went up to his face and he felt the old urge to
run away.

"Ega! Weege!" the youngster screamed, and in no
time Rico and Mike were surrounded by jostling, jabber-
ing, naked children. Their faces were flat, their noses
broad with flaring nostrils, and their hair fell long and
unkempt. No two were the same color. Some were as
fair as Mike and some had pink eyes like white rabbits.
All had the coarse hair of the Indian, but one child's hair
was the color of corn silk, another's was brown, and still
others had hair of a reddish cast. A few had hair that
was almost colorless.

"They look like Indians and still they don't," Mike
said, awe in his voice at the strangeness of these people.

Rico was taller than most of the Indian children and over their heads he saw the chief hand the birds to Uncle Thomáso. "Let's move over to our own camp," he said.

Every Indian child tagged along.

"My dad came to study the White Indians," Mike laughed, "but they're studying us instead."

"Does your father just want to look at the Indians?" Rico asked.

"Oh, no. Tomorrow he'll take pictures, measure their heads, the length of their thigh bones, check the way their teeth fit together, and all sorts of things. He'll write it all down."

"Why?" Rico asked.

"It's a scientific way of telling what race people belong to," Mike explained.

It still seemed silly to Rico. "Do your teeth fit like mine?"

Mike bared his teeth and Rico did the same. Both sets met evenly in front and they laughed at each other, much to the delight of the watching children, who mimicked and laughed, too.

"In some people, the upper teeth fit over the lowers differently," Mike said.

"What difference does it make? Don't they work just the same?" Rico asked.

"Sure," Mike said, "but it has nothing to do with the use."

Rico gave up. He didn't understand it, but if Professor Davis and Mike had come all this way, there must be something to it.

Uncle Thomáso came over scolding because he couldn't fix dinner in such confusion. Professor Davis was too absorbed to notice. He was looking at each Indian as if he had been offered many presents and couldn't decide which one to open first.

Finally the visiting chief brought over a tall,

strongly-built White Indian whose hair was lighter than all the others and whose eyes were of pale gray. The black and red lines painted on his fair skin were like waves and he walked with a flowing motion. Immediately all the other Indians fell back. The White Indian stopped in front of each guest, then went back to stand beside the other chief. He began to talk in a commanding rhythm.

"He is welcoming us to his poor home," Uncle Thomáso said, "and explaining that he is not prepared to offer us a feast, but that he will be happy to do so tomorrow if we will remain."

"Thank the chief for his kindness, but tell him we cannot impose upon his generosity. Say that we have come to make a study of his people."

When the exchange had been completed, the chief said goodnight and turned to his people. He spoke briefly and they all moved away to their homes. Soon an Indian boy brought another torch made of small, round

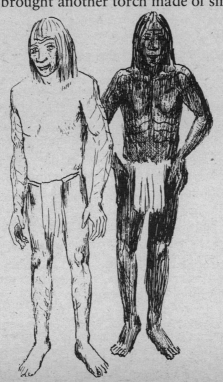

nuts strung on a sharpened stick. As one nut burned out it lighted the next one so that the camp was as bright as when the kerosene lantern burned.

Uncle Thomáso served supper. "It's better than turkey at home," Mike said, and Rico thought that his mother cooked few things that tasted better. Rico was about to take another bite when he thought about something. "If the dart is poison, how can we eat the meat?" he asked Uncle Thomáso.

"It hasn't hurt the Indians," Uncle Thomáso laughed, "and they have been hunting that way for centuries. It isn't real poison. It's an herb on the tip of the dart that only paralyzes the bird so the Indian can catch him."

"Quit spoiling my supper," Mike said, and he reached for a drumstick. "Rico always asks why and I just want to eat."

Professor Davis laughed. "A little more 'why' might save you trouble sometime," he said to his son.

"Maybe," Mike laughed back, "but not now," and he took another big bite of meat.

Later, when the boys were lying side by side in the dark, Mike whispered, "I hope we get to explore those ruins."

Rico was only half listening. He, too, was thinking about a visit to the ruins. So far, it was his best lead to finding the medicine men.

"I read in a book about a fellow finding gold in an old ruin. It had been hidden there by Indians to keep the Spanish from taking it."

"But the chief said 'bruja'," Rico said to discourage Mike.

"That's only silly superstition," Mike went on. "There's no such thing as witches or evil spirits. Everybody knows that."

Rico wasn't sure. Besides, he had his own plans. So while Mike talked on and on, Rico fell sound asleep.

100

Chapter Twelve

Rico opened his eyes to look squarely into the pink ones of a White Indian boy whose hand was tracing the patterns of his scar. Other children were crowded around, watching. "No!" Rico exploded and flopped over on his side.

The children vanished, but it was no use trying to go to sleep again. They swarmed over the camp and Rico heard Uncle Thomáso mutter as he tried to cook breakfast. When Rico rolled from his bed, the children were gone.

Breakfast was a short meal. Professor Davis was anxious to begin his study. "We'll set up our station in front of the camp," he announced, "and rope off a section with vines so that only one Indian comes in at a time. Can you take down my information?" The professor was speaking to Rico's father, who nodded and immediately went to cut the vines.

"We'll need three or four wood blocks to set things on," he added. "The Indians can probably lend them to us."

Uncle Thomáso went off for the blocks while Professor Davis unpacked a tape measure and other things Rico had never seen.

"Michael, you and Rico can work with your camera. We'll need some good candid shots of the White Indian children."

Mike immediately pulled his pack from beneath his cot and got out his camera. "First, I want a good picture of you, Rico," he said, putting the strap around his neck and checking the camera.

"No!" Rico's answer was loud and forceful.

His father stopped cutting vines in the jungle growth along the edge of the camp, and Uncle Thomáso dropped a wooden block. They all looked at Rico in surprise. He felt ashamed and angry, but he couldn't say anything. He didn't want Mike to show his friends a picture of his twisted face.

"I'm sorry, Rico." It was Mike who understood immediately.

The others went back to their work and, for a few minutes, the boys stood around. Then Rico grabbed up a stake his father brought in and drove it into the ground to help build the enclosure. Mike joined in and by the time the job was done, Rico felt better.

If his face were fixed he wouldn't mind if Mike took a picture. He started wondering how he could slip away alone to the ruins. He'd have to be sure his father wouldn't miss him and set up a search.

When the White Chief came over to see how he could help, Professor Davis said, "Tell the chief I would be honored if he would be our first subject."

The professor opened the notebook and explained his methods to Rico's father, who wrote down the words and figures under their proper headings as the professor called them out.

Rico and Mike stood by while a comment on every part of the White Chief's body was noted in the book. After the chief, one Indian after another came in to be measured. The boys grew restless. Rico still couldn't make sense of it. What difference if a man were six feet tall like Professor Davis, or less than five feet as were most of the Indians?

By this time the children were back, pushing and arguing to get closest to the enclosure. "Let's try for some pictures," Mike said. "See that boy with white skin and dirty-looking white hair? He sure doesn't look like an Indian."

They went over to the boy, showed him the camera and motioned him to stand away from the other children. Immediately all the others were curious and had to be shown. But as soon as Mike pointed his camera at the boy, he ran away. Mike went to his pack and brought out a picture postcard to try to show what he wanted. The children nodded, fingered the picture and the camera, but still ran off as soon as Mike tried to focus.

When sunlight flooded the clearing, the White Indians vanished into their huts, leaving the boys without a single picture. "They'll never let you point the camera if they can see it," Mike said. "The only way is to take pictures when they don't know it."

"But how can we do that?" Rico wanted to know. "They're all over the place."

After some discussion, the boys decided to build a hiding place in a spot where Mike could set up his camera and take pictures without being seen. Rico's job would be to get the children into Mike's line of vision.

When the afternoon siesta was over, Mike was waiting in his hiding place. Rico got some small pieces of paper and three pencils from Mr. Davis. He walked over to the Indian village and brought back three blocks. On each one, carefully placed, he put a pencil and paper. Sitting with his back to the camera, he began to draw pictures. Right away an Indian boy wanted to try. Rico got up and placed the paper so that the boy faced the camera as he tried to use the pencil. Rico stood back and watched the face of each child as he tried his skill with a pencil. Mike's camera sounded one click after another, and Rico knew their scheme had worked.

He was watching when he heard another sound. "A-EE, A-ee, A-EE." It was the shrill whistling call of the three-toed sloth, only it went on and on instead of stopping and starting as the sloth's call usually sounded.

Rico was not far from the trail and as he listened, he was sure he heard a shuffling sound as of hurried

footsteps. He looked toward their camp but his father, Professor Davis, and Uncle Thomáso were all absorbed in the business of measuring the White Indians.

Rico was uncertain. Were the Indians plotting something and was the call of the sloth a signal? He knew they were a simple people and he had heard many stories of their superstitions. Had they unknowingly made the Indians angry?

The sound was now a compelling call. Without considering further, Rico made his way to the trail and stealthily moved ahead. The closed-in jungle path was dark after the open campsite and at first he saw nothing. He walked faster and as he came around a curve in the trail, he saw the White Chief not fifty feet ahead.

Rico stopped. He was afraid to go farther. He knew that an Indian would not wait to ask who or why. He would shoot. Already Rico could feel the sharp points of the poison darts pierce his skin. He was thinking about it so hard that he was surprised to see the chief still walking forward on the trail.

Rico slipped down on his hands and knees without making a sound. Working carefully, he moved the jungle growth at the side of the path until he had made a nest for himself. He lay down in it, his head facing the trail, and pulled the growth closer in front of him. Gradually he eased forward so that he had an opening to watch the White Chief ahead. Rico saw him stop as two Indians of normal skin tone came toward him from the opposite direction. The White Indian took something from one of them and turned to retrace his steps.

Rico edged back into his nest and made an opening higher from the ground so that he would not be noticed. As the chief came close, Rico saw that he was carrying in his arms a boy of about four years old, whose hair was the color of Mike's and whose face and body were red and raw-looking. Rico couldn't see the color of the child's eyes. A string of shiny nose rings, like those worn by the women, dangled from the chief's belt. The child was crying and the chief was talking to him in a low voice as he walked along.

Rico lay where he was until he was sure the chief was back in his own village. He thought better of going to the old ruins now that he had seen the newcomers go back in that direction. Slowly he eased back onto the trail and walked to camp. He was disappointed and discouraged. At this rate, he'd never get a chance to go to the ruins alone.

By the time Rico returned, the professor was putting away his notes. "Where have you been?" he asked.

Rico told him what he had seen. Professor Davis jumped from his wood block. "I knew it! I knew it!" His voice rang with satisfaction and he got out his black notebook again.

Rico could make no sense of the professor's excitement and finally wandered over to the Indian village hoping to learn the meaning of what he had just seen. Mike tagged along, but Rico hardly heard his chatter about photographing the children.

The village was as sorry looking as on the day they had arrived, only now there were at least two dogs in front of each hut. From the chief's house came a thin cry and the crooning voice of a woman. They went back to their camp.

"Thomáso," Professor Davis was saying, "after dinner will you bring the White Chief? I want to ask him some questions."

When the White Chief sat on a block opposite Professor Davis, Uncle Thomáso translated as best he could.

"Tell the chief we are most grateful for his help and I would like him to have my machete as a token of appreciation."

The chief took the new machete and, without a word,

walked over to a small tree and slashed. Satisfied, he came back, smiled, and nodded many times. Then he took his old machete from his belt and fastened on the new one. Rico noticed that the old one was so worn from sharpening that it looked more like a dagger than a machete.

Professor Davis began again. "Tell the chief my studies indicate that the White Indians are not a separate tribe. Ask him if that is correct."

"We are Indians," was the answer.

Professor Davis tried another question. Suddenly, while Uncle Thomáso was trying to make him understand, the chief jumped up, motioned, and went off to his hut.

"What struck him?" Mike wondered.

"I think he'll come back," Rico said, and as they talked, the White Chief came toward them carrying the child Rico had seen him accept earlier that day.

"He came today," Uncle Thomáso said, after listening to the chief.

"Ask if children come from many tribes," the professor prompted Uncle Thomáso.

The Indian began to talk, and when the long speech had ended, Uncle Thomáso explained. "He says all tribes sometimes have White Indian babies. They are not strong and cannot live like others. And, if they were to survive, they would eventually weaken the whole tribe. So all the tribes bring their pink-skinned children here to be cared for. In payment, the White Indians are left alone and their hunting grounds are not used by other tribes."

Thomáso paused and after some thought he added, "The chief says the tribes bring presents, too, that they love their children and bring them here only because they know that the tribe must be kept strong if it is to survive."

Professor Davis stood up smiling. He had the answer to the riddle of the White Indians. He bowed to the chief and said to Thomáso, "Tell the chief he is doing a great favor to the world and that I thank him for his help."

When the chief had gone, the professor turned to Rico. "If you hadn't seen the White Chief pick up the baby, I would not have the answer to the origin of the White Indians."

As always when he was praised, Rico could find nothing to say.

"I feel sorry for the kids," Mike said.

"Yes," the professor agreed, "but they are better off here. You saw how the child's face and body were burned and sore from exposure to the sun. These people are the Albino children of many Indian tribes."

But why aren't they like the other Indians if they're born the same?" Rico asked.

"We don't know that, Rico, but we do know that some people are born with little or no color in their skin and in the colored part of their eyes. Their bodies can't tolerate strong light, and they can't live as other Indians do."

Rico walked over to stand beside his father. He was thinking of the little boy taken away from his mother and father when he was so small. "Are there lots of people like the White Indians?" he asked.

"No," Professor Davis answered. "In some countries an Albino is rarely found, but there are more of them among the Indians in this part of the world than any other place."

Rico was quiet. He was trying to decide which was the worst handicap—the isolated life of an Indian Albino, or the personal thorn of living with a disfigured face. "I'm glad I'm not an Albino," Rico said softly.

Chapter Thirteen

The next morning Professor Davis studied the children. It was Rico's and Mike's job to select those who would be allowed in the enclosure. Every child wanted to be measured. Mike started the game of drawing straws and the youngsters laughed and accepted the method good-naturedly. When the sun drove the White Indians to shelter, Professor Davis announced that he would spend the rest of the day working on his notes.

"We might look around for ivory nuts," Uncle Thomáso suggested to Rico's father. "They grow bigger up here than in the lower country."

The two boys were left to themselves and, at Mike's suggestion, they decided to go exploring. "How about those ruins we saw in the jungle?" Mike asked. "Let's go there."

Rico shook his head. "The chief said 'bruja,' so we'd better stay away from there." He didn't tell Mike that he preferred to be by himself when he went there.

"Why not?" Mike insisted. "There's no such thing as spirits. If they are Spanish ruins, the Indians wouldn't go near because they hated the Spaniards."

"My father wouldn't like it," Rico said.

"We'll only stay a little while," Mike persisted, and started toward the trail. Rico hesitated for a moment and then hurried after him. It might be his only chance to look there for the medicine men.

As they came in sight of the ruins, Rico stepped ahead and began slashing with his machete. "I'll clear the way," he said.

"I'd like to be able to handle a machete like that,"

Mike said. Rico didn't answer, but went on clearing a path. "The rocks feel hot all the way through the soles of my shoes," Mike said.

They wandered from one pile of stones to another. Heat rose from the rocks in waves. Mike stopped to pull his shirt away from his damp back. "It must have been a big camp to have had so many stone buildings," he said. "I wonder what it was for."

Rico didn't answer. His interest in the ruins stemmed from his hope that some of the medicine men might live there. But as they continued to explore, he realized that it was no longer a fit dwelling place for any humans.

"Look," Mike said, pointing to a platform made of gigantic beams. "Maybe there's something under it."

They climbed down to look, and Mike hurried around the platform. At one corner he saw an opening where a slab of stone had slipped away. Vines crowded around the opening, but it looked big enough to get through. Without hesitating, Mike lowered himself into the opening.

Before Rico could follow after him, Mike let out a terrifying scream. Then there was a loud thud, and silence. With one leap, Rico followed after Mike.

It was dark in the cavern, but as his eyes adjusted he saw Mike lying on the ground struggling to defend himself against an angry ocelot, who clawed and tore at him.

Rico's blood pounded in his head. His first thought was that the cat's mate might be near and ready to pounce. The ocelot was so intent that it didn't see or smell him. Abruptly, before Rico could decide what to do, the cat stopped clawing Mike and slowly circled him. Mike had stopped struggling, and lay still. The long black circles on the cat's gray-gold coat quivered, and its strong hind paws threw up clouds of choking dust. Rico knew that ocelots were fierce in the jungle, but he was

111

used to his gentle pet at home, and this killer-cat un-
nerved him. Then he knew what he had to do.

He dug his feet into the earth and grasped his machete
in both hands and raised it. When the ocelot came even
with him, he brought it down at the head of the animal
with all his strength. The sound bounced back at him
from the stones in the walls, and for a split second, he felt
weak and drained. The ocelot halted, then swung
around to face him. Its wild, yellow eyes jerked Rico
back to reality. The cat hunched down to spring. Rico
jumped at it and again crashed his machete on its head.
Blood spurted, and the animal lost consciousness and
fell against Mike.

Rico stood still for a moment, his machete grasped
tightly in his hands. He felt sick in his stomach from the
acid stench of fresh blood, and his body trembled. Sweat
ran down his nose and he wiped it off with his arm.
Mike hadn't stirred.

"Mike," Rico whispered hoarsely, sinking to his
knees beside his friend. When there was no response,
Rico forgot his need to watch out for other ocelots
nearby and began dragging Mike out of the cavern.
Half-pulling and half-lifting, he managed to get him out.
"Wake up, Mike," he called out urgently. "You've got
to help!"

There was no answer. Mike lay still. Blood oozed
from the claw marks on his face and stained his clothes.
Straining every muscle, Rico lifted Mike in his arms and
stumbled a few steps. The trail they had cut was narrow,
and he couldn't see where he was going. Mike was too
heavy to carry this way. Gently he set him on the ground
and leaned over. "Can't you walk just a little, Mike?" he
pleaded.

Still there was no answer. Fear choked Rico. What if
Mike died before he could get him to camp? "I can't
carry you in my arms," Rico said aloud, and looked up
at the sound of his own voice.

Realizing that he had forgotten his machete, Rico forced himself back into the underground cavern, grabbed it up, and ran out without looking around him. Only one idea was clear. Somehow, he'd have to get Mike to camp. "Help me, God. Please help me," he begged.

Rico stood puzzling, his eyes on the ground. Then his eyes focussed on the liana vines. He collected several stout ones, all the while thinking about how he could tie Mike to his back. With vines in hand, he noticed a stump near where Mike lay. He cut notches in it with his machete and laid a vine in each notch. Next he dragged Mike and propped him against the stump and brought the vines around him, spreading the ends within reach so that he could draw them around his body when he got Mike on his back. Kneeling between Mike's outspread legs, with his back against Mike's stomach, he drew the vines tightly around his own body. It took every bit of his strength to get to his feet. He grabbed the stump to steady himself and looked ahead at the route he must take back to camp. The sight of the ocelot's cave jarred him into action. Still staggering, he stumbled forward.

Rico forgot the heat and the many flies that swarmed over him. His only thought was to keep going until he reached camp. When his eyes blurred, he raked his hand across them to wipe off the sweat. His mind and his whole body felt numb. Only his feet went forward. He dared not rest. If he stopped, he feared he would never be able to start again. Mike might die. A snake slithered across the path. He paid no attention. Any other time, he would have watched to be sure it wasn't a poisonous snake. He started to tremble and for a while he grabbed trees to the sides of the path to keep himself steady.

When he reached the edge of the village, the frightened cries of the Indian children brought older people. He paid no attention. He had to get into camp. When he

saw Professor Davis running toward him, he went weak with relief and would have fallen but for strong supporting arms.

The professor quickly cut the vines and carried Mike into camp. Rico sank down as if he had been supported and the prop had been knocked from beneath him. No one paid any attention to him. They had all followed Professor Davis.

Rico didn't know how long he sat without feeling and without thought. The chatter of the excited Indians was only a wave of sound flowing over him. Suddenly, Uncle Thomáso was holding water to his lips, and his father's arm was around his shoulders. Rico drank. Then the need to know about Mike overcame his weariness. With the slowness of one who had been ill a long time, he got to his feet.

"What happened?" Uncle Thomáso asked.

"We went to explore some ruins. An ocelot was underneath. It knocked Mike down. I killed it." Rico felt too tired to say another word.

"I'll carry you in," Uncle Thomáso offered.

Rico shook his head. He staggered forward and his father said gently, "Steady, son," and took his arm to help while Uncle Thomáso pushed through the Indians to camp.

Mike lay on a cot, his naked body still caked with blood. The professor was bending over him, cleaning and bandaging the wounds. Rico sank down and watched silently. Mike lay with his eyes closed and did not move.

When Mr. Davis could do no more, he came and stood near Rico. The worry lines were deep in his forehead and his eyes were anxious. "Tell me what happened, Rico," he said. His voice was gentle.

Rico swallowed hard. "We went to explore some ruins," he said in a choked voice.

The professor looked at Mike and then at Rico's face. To Rico it was an accusing look; it said that it was his fault that Mike had been attacked.

"It was my fault," he said miserably. "We shouldn't have gone."

The still form on the cot moved slightly. Professor Davis was holding a spoonful of water to Mike's lips before Rico realized what had happened. Mike opened his eyes and struggled to speak. "Not Rico's fault," he whispered weakly.

Rico looked at Professor Davis. His eyes were blurred and his lips moved silently and Rico knew that he was praying.

The professor's voice interrupted his thoughts. "Drink this, Rico," he said, "and rest. Michael's going to be all right. We'll hear the whole story later."

Rico looked at Professor Davis. In a strained, choked voice he asked, "Will Mike's face be scarred like mine?"

Professor Davis put his arm around Rico's shoulders. "I think not, Rico," he said. "Mike's face has been badly scratched, but the wounds aren't deep enough to leave permanent scars."

Rico's eyes lighted with relief and he straightened his shoulders. His hand moved over his scarred face. Then he held both his hands out and studied them with intent. "My face," he said slowly, as if speaking to himself, "it is scarred and ugly. But my hands," and he held them toward the professor with pride, "they are strong."

ico, are you awake?" Mike whispered into the darkness.

"Yes," Rico whispered back. "I'm not sleepy anymore." There was silence. Far off a cat howled and Rico shivered at the sound. Then a great loneliness came over him. In a day or two, they would be going home, and he'd be back to the same old routine of making charcoal and delivering it to Maria Blanca. If medicine men existed who could make his face well, he hadn't found them.

Mike would be gone—the only friend who had understood how he felt about his face. Mike liked him for himself, and didn't even think about his scars. Mike didn't even remember them when he had wanted to take Rico's picture.

The next thing Rico knew, Mike was poking him with his bandaged hand. "Shhh!" he whispered.

Rico half listened. The chatter of the Indians and of their parents flowed over him like a wave. The chief was talking to Professor Davis while Uncle Thomáso translated, and some of their conversation was lost in the noise.

Mike prodded him again. "The Indians are planning a ceremony to honor you."

Light was filtering into the clearing. Wide awake and curious now, Rico listened to the professor.

"Mike tells me that more than anything else, Rico wants to have a smooth face like other boys."

Rico's senses leaped to attention.

"More than once he has saved Michael's life, and if it hadn't been for him, I might never have been able to prove that the White Indians are Albinos. We would like to repay our debt to him."

Rico heard his father draw his breath sharply, but Professor Davis talked on. "The university where I teach has a medical school that is well-known for its work in plastic surgery. Since Rico's scar is an old one, I don't know how much success we might expect, but with your consent, I would like to look into this."

Rico's feelings almost choked him. Could doctors make his face smooth again? He turned toward the voices and saw Professor Davis, his father, and Uncle Thomáso sitting around the campfire drinking coffee. As he watched, Professor Davis got up and brought the pot over to refill the cups. Still Rico's father said nothing. He sat with his head down staring at the ground, the cup unnoticed in his hand.

"You need have no worry about the boy," Professor Davis said. "He would have fine care in our home. I'm sure he and Michael would be good for each other."

Rico thought he couldn't bear it another minute if his father didn't speak. He saw his uncle reach down and pick up a twig and crush it in his fingers, but his father sat

119

quietly. After a long silence, he raised his hand and brought it across his eyes as if to clear his vision. "It would be hard to have the boy away," he began.

Uncle Thomáso got up impatiently. "How you feel about that makes no difference," he said bluntly. "It's how the boy will go through life that counts."

"Yes, yes. Of course," his father said, as if coming from a long distance. Then, turning directly to Professor Davis, he said, "Thank you, Señor, thank you. A normal life for my boy . . .," his voice choked with feeling, ". . . it is the greatest of all gifts."

In wonder Rico realized that it was his father's love for him that was struggling to accept a separation.

"We are plain people who live by hard work," his father went on, as if thinking aloud. "Would my boy be satisfied to come back to our simple jungle life after he has lived with the riches of your great country?"

"It is every man's right to choose the life he wants," Uncle Thomáso muttered.

"Yes," Rico's father said slowly. "There would be many things to work out, but we will see how we can manage if your doctors can help."

Rico jumped from his bed and ran out to his father, who put his arm around his son's shoulders. "So you heard the professor's offer," he said.

Rico could not speak. But there was no need for words now.

It was a long day. Mike rested and Rico wandered about. Shortly before evening, Rico saw the little boy that the White Chief had taken into their tribe. He was sitting with a motherly woman, laughing and pointing to children playing near. Already his flesh had lost the look of rawness.

"*That's* what Old Indian Pete meant!" Rico exclaimed to himself. "The *Moon Men* are the White Indians. They heal and care for those born without enough coloring in their skins." Rico laughed out loud, thinking how stupid he had been not to have realized this before.

Soon the beat of the skin drum throbbed through the dark clearing. Pebble-filled gourds rattled an accompaniment. The chief led his men into the visitor's camp, their flaming torches hissing. He stopped before Rico, who rose and stood solemnly, compelled by the other's dignity. They all circled the clearing to stop where a seat of honor had been set apart for Rico. The rest of his party were at one side, and the Indians squatted in front of him according to their tribal rank. Then the chief moved up beside Rico and, in words and motions, acted out Rico's deed in killing the ocelot.

The chief stepped back and Rico looked into the faces before him. They were looking at him with respect and affection. Instinctively he started to lift his hand to cover the scarred side of his face. Then he let it fall, realizing that no one was looking at him in horror or in revulsion, but with admiration and friendliness. His father's words to his mother came back to him, "The boy has to learn to live with his scarred face. He can't always run away." The words had sounded cruel to him before, but now Rico began to understand what his father had meant. It wasn't a man's looks that determined his worth—it was how he thought about things—and people—and about himself, too. And right now, he felt better about himself

than he ever had before. It would be good to have his face fixed, but the scars were old and the professor had left room for doubt. But it didn't matter as much now as it had before he'd made the trip into the mountains. Now he could live with himself and be with people without shrinking away from them.

When the ceremony had ended, the chief handed Rico an ivory nut carved in the form of an ocelot.

Rico ran to Uncle Thomáso. "Tell the chief," he said, "tell him . . . ," Rico faltered, "tell him that I said thank you."

Uncle Thomáso spoke for a long time. When he had finished, the chief touched Rico on the forehead, turned, and led his men back to the village. Rico didn't have to be told that the gesture made it his right to march beside the chief.

The entire village saw them off the next day. It was easier going down the mountain than it had been coming up, although Mike needed frequent rests.

When they arrived at home, mama noticed right away the change in Rico. She saw how direct his gaze was now, and how straight and proud he carried himself. Something good had happened to him on the trip, and her heart sang with the gladness of it.

"We have much to tell you, Mama," Rico said, and he put his arm around her. The expression in his eyes told her all that she needed to know.

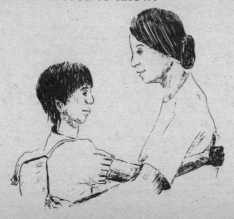

ABOUT THE AUTHOR

Mary Louise Sherer grew up in Idaho in a mining family, and married a mining engineer. She has made her home at a gold camp in California and near lead and silver mines in Japan, Korea and China. Before her marriage she was graduated from the University of Idaho and taught English and typing to Hawaiian students at a boy's high school in Honolulu. Presently she lives east of Seattle, Washington, on the shores of Lake Sammamish in a stone house which she and her late husband built themselves.

ABOUT THE ARTIST

Beverly Dobrin Wallace studied printmaking at Pratt Graphics Art Center in New York City and painting and design at Carnegie Tech in Pittsburgh, Pennsylvania, where she grew up. Her work has been shown in New York galleries and in national exhibits. She is a graduate of Hofstra University in New York, from which she holds a Master's degree. She has taught art in elementary schools in New York in Commack and Somers. Currently she is teaching art as occupational therapy to geriatric patients at a New York hospital. Mrs. Wallace lives with her husband and her two sons in a century-old farmhouse in Mahopac, New York.